Misfit McCabe

by

LK Gardner-Griffie

This book is dedicated to my sister Dana. She inspired me to write something for the age group we now identify as "tweens"; those who still have both feet firmly in childhood, but are actively looking forward to the exciting phase of being a teenager.

The journey of this book started many years ago, and I am happy to be able to brush the dust off, give it a final few tweaks, and launch it at long last.

Thanks to Pam, Gail, and Diane for helping me fine tune the work. Special thanks to Keely, Emily, Madeleine, and Leo for being the enthusiastic classroom readers and for providing feedback.

Misfit McCabe

ISBN 978-4357-0405-3

Misfit McCabe
Table of Contents

Cast of Characters

Katie McCabe   A fourteen year old rebel with a history of trying to run away from home. She is sent to live with relatives and is determined to cause as many problems as she can.

Sam McCabe   Katie's father and the sheriff of a microscopic town. He was the youngest of seven brothers who spread the McCabe reputation far and wide. The hardest decision he ever had to make was the one to send Katie to live with his brother.

Charley McCabe   The oldest of the McCabe brothers, he runs a construction company and owns a small farm. A strict disciplinarian, Katie sees his softer side when she needs it most.

Matthew McCabe   Charley's oldest son who reminds Katie of her own father, especially when times get tough.

Mark McCabe   Resembling his own father more, Mark has more of a rebel spirit that Katie can identify with.

Sarah McCabe   A daughter of one of the other McCabe brothers, she came to live with Uncle Charley eleven years ago. She helps Katie deal with all of the changes in her life.

Cast of Characters

Timmy Lawrence Katie's best friend and partner in crime. Wherever trouble was found, the two of them would be together.

Harriet Denton Sarah's friend and employer, she owns a gift shop downtown.

H.L. Denton He owns the bank and most of the businesses in town and his son doesn't let anyone forget it.

Harvey Denton, Jr. A peer of Katie's who takes pleasure in trying to make her angry. A contest of revenge develops between the two.

Jim Baines A deputy sheriff and Sarah's boyfriend. He catches Katie when she is breaking the law.

Tom Pike A High School Junior and member of the football team, Tom is Katie's first friend in town, and wants to make sure he's the best one.

Emma Carter The only person at school who can stand Harvey's presence for any length of time. When Tom shows his interest in Katie, Emma conspires with Harvey to frame Katie for something she didn't do.

The Burning Shed

"You know I'll swear it was all my idea."

"But, Katie, it was all your idea." Tim reached behind his back and pulled out a flask. "Except for this."

"Are you getting sly on me, Timmy Lawrence?" He never tried anything without checking it out with me first. "What's in it?" Other than something to get us both into trouble.

He shrugged one shoulder and leaned back against the side of the shed. "Oh, nothing much. Just a little rum to go with the cokes I brought." He cracked open a can and handed it to me. "Drink some out, so I can spice it up for you."

Swallowing as much as I could in a mouthful, I passed the can back to him. "What made you think of this?" A new Timmy was emerging, and I didn't know exactly how to handle him.

He grinned as he concentrated on pouring the rum into the coke. "I just figured that if we were going to start smoking, we might as well mark the occasion with a drink of celebration." He doctored his drink and set the flask on the ground. "Anyway, you're always saying that I never come up with my own ideas. So I did."

"I'll say. And what an idea." I could see the faint flush of pride on Tim's cheeks.

Although the afternoon sun shone brightly, the inside of the shed remained dark. The only light filtered through the cracks in the walls. We kept the light off in order to keep from attracting any attention, not that we would. Even with the lights on and the door open, the shed was hidden from the house and people were used to seeing me on the property because I helped Mr. Pickford with the care of his animals.

Tim held up his can. "Cheers."

I jumped off the hay bale to click cans with his and accidentally knocked the flask over. "Oh Timmy, I'm sorry." I grabbed it and stood it up again. "I only spilled a little." Nervously, I looked up at his face.

"Forget it. I should have put the cap back on." He held his can back up in the air. "To our adventure in smoking."

This time we clinked without mishap and I took a big swig of my drink. It sent shivers up and down my spine and my face felt flushed. Having watched other smokers do it, I smacked the pack of cigarettes on my palm and took two out. Sticking one in the corner of my mouth, I handed the other to Tim. "Light me up."

Timmy tore out a match. "Just a warning, my dad smokes strong ones." He struck the match and it flared up. "Here you go." He held the burning match toward me.

Not wanting to gag, I didn't inhale all the way on my first puff. I had an image to preserve. Timmy struck another match and held it to the end of his cigarette. Though he tried not to, he started to cough. I took another drag, a little deeper this time. I figured I could work my way up to really smoking. I picked up the matches Tim dropped.

"It's really interesting how people get engrossed in watching a flame." I lit one and stared at it while it flickered. Right before it burned my fingers I shook it out and dropped it. Lighting another, I held it in front of Tim's eyes. "What do you think about when you stare at it?"

He gazed at it without answering. Watching his face, I wondered about our changing relationship. Timmy had been my best friend for as long as I could remember, but now he wanted more and I wasn't sure I did. Both of us were fourteen and not really understanding the changes we were going through. "Ouch!" I flung the match away from me as it burned my fingers. I looked over to where it fell to make sure it had gone out. I turned back and looked into Timmy's gray eyes. "So, what do you thing about when you stare at a flame?"

Tim stroked his jaw and gave a little half shrug. "I don't know, I think I kind of stop thinking when I stare at a flame. It just mesmerizes me." Timmy moved over to sit next to me on the hay bale. "Katie, are you still going to be friends with me once we start high school?"

What kind of question was that? "Of course we'll still be friends. You're my best friend, and nothing, not even starting a new school, is going to change that." I bumped my shoulder against his. "Don't be ridiculous."

Timmy looked down at his sneakers as they kicked up against the hay bale we sat on. "I just thought you might make all sorts of new friends, and wouldn't need me for a friend to hang out with anymore."

"Hey, look at me." Timmy gave me sideways glance. "If any new so-called friends are not friends with you too, then I don't need them. Any new friends I have will want to be friends with you. You are a great guy and don't let anyone tell you any differently."

As Tim started to straighten up, I heard a crackling sound behind me. As he turned to look at me his eyes got big and all of a sudden I could smell smoke overpowering the smell of the cigarettes. The dry hay had caught fire. It must have started from the match I thought had gone out, and the flames were starting to rage. Grabbing Timmy's hand, I followed my instincts and ran.

Running as fast as I could, I wanted to get as far away as possible. I noticed that somehow I lost Tim. Turning around, I saw him looking back at the shed. "Timmy! Come on! We have got to get out of here."

Tim shook his head. "Katie, we have to try and put it out."

"Are you crazy? If we stick around here, we'll get caught." We didn't even have anything to put it out with. But, he did have a point. If we let it go, it would burn down more than just the shed. Mr. Pickford's entire farm would be at risk, as well as the whole town, if it got out of control. "How are we going to put it out? It'll be burned down by the time I can get a pail of water back here."

"How should I know? You're supposed to be the brainy one with all the bright ideas."

Timmy sounded angry, but I knew it was fear talking. And I didn't blame him, I was scared too. "Okay, I'm thinking." Or trying to. "We gotta call the fire department." Brilliant. "Run to the nearest phone and call. Say we were just passing by or something." Please, whatever you do, don't say I set the place on fire. "Then see if you can get a shovel and get back here as fast as you can." I could have saved my breath on the last comment because Timmy was already gone.

I turned around and faced the burning shed once more trying to determine if there was anything I could do while waiting for help to come. At least I couldn't see the flames outside yet. Running over to a young tree, I broke off a long, leafy branch. I placed my hands on the outside of the shed door to feel for heat. It was still cool. Stepping to one side of the door, I balanced on one foot and kicked the door in. I jumped back. No flames came shooting out. That was a good sign. I looked inside. Almost the entire floor was engulfed in flames. I started beating those closest to me.

Sweating from the intense heat, I kept beating the flames in a losing battle. My eyes and throat stung from the smoke and I felt like help would never come. After I singed the first branch completely, I ran back and got another branch and continued beating the flames the best I could.

"Help is on the way!" Timmy thrust a shovel into my hands. "Someone should be here any minute."

I threw the branch away and began shoveling dirt on to the flames. Someone better come in a hurry. I beat the fire the best I could, but it was still burning more than Timmy and I could control. I drew my arm across my face in an attempt to keep the sweat from running into my eyes.

Part of the shed wall caught fire and I concentrated on trying to get that out. My lungs burned from the smoke and I began to cough with each thrust of the shovel. The stinging of my eyes gave way to blurred vision from the combination of sweat and smoke. My head ached and I started to feel lightheaded.

In the distance a siren sounded and I felt a sense of relief. In moments we were surrounded by the helpers of the volunteer fire department. Thank goodness the whole shed was not in flames. In what seemed like minutes, the fire was out.

I jammed my shovel into the ground and took a deep breath of the char scented air.

"Katherine Elizabeth McCabe!"

Daddy. My heart seemed to stop and I got a sick feeling in the pit of my stomach. I braced myself before turning around. "Hi, Dad." I should have known that he would have to show up. "Little bit of a fire, wouldn't you say?"

He frowned. "What did you have to do with this?"

"I can't believe it. You automatically assume that I had something to do with the fire." Maybe if I played enough of the injured innocent, he would believe it. "You don't ever give me the benefit of the doubt."

Placing his hands on his hips, his blue eyes pierced straight into mine. "Are you through with that nonsense?"

He definitely didn't buy it. "All right! I'm guilty." I shot my arms straight in front of me. "Cuff me and take me away." I would be better off in jail than if he took me home, that was for sure. At least at the jail, he'd be on the other side of the bars.

Grabbing my wrists, he pulled me away from the crowd. Struggling to maintain some of my dignity, I yanked my wrists from his grasp. Sparks seemed to kindle in his blue eyes. "You will keep a civil tongue in your head." His anger was on a tight reign. "Half of the town is congregated here, and you have to show how little respect you hold for me and my position as sheriff. I've had enough."

Oops. I definitely overstepped my boundaries this time. I couldn't look him in the face. "I'm sorry." Barely able to mumble the apology, I steeled myself for the questions that were sure to come.

His square jaw set as he took a deep breath. "How did the fire start?" The question came almost gently, but then restrained anger came through. "And, I don't want any padding to make yourself or anyone else look better." His middle two fingers rubbed the area between his eyebrows, the way they did every time he got really perturbed with me. "I also know that whatever happened, Tim was right there with you."

In other words, don't alter the facts. I'd say one thing for my dad, he sure knew me well. And he never gave me an inch. "It all started as a kind of experiment."

He raised an eyebrow. "Tell it straight."

I couldn't look into his eyes anymore. "I wanted to try smoking and convinced Timmy that we'd look real cool if we learned how." Daddy would blow sky high with this one. "So we met in Mr. Pickford's shed, and when I was goofing around with the matches, I lit some hay on fire." Daddy's silence became ominous. The quieter Daddy got, the more trouble I would be in. "Then, I guess I panicked. I should have put it out then, but I ran instead."

I couldn't bring myself to tell him about the rum. He'd have a heart attack or something. "Everything in there was so dry the fire was out of control in no time." Would a few tears at this point help my case? Not a chance. Anyway, why cheapen myself. "Timmy and I did everything we could. I'm sorry."

The silence deepened for a moment. "Katie, you need to apologize to Mr. Pickford. . ." My favorite thing to do in the world. ". . .and tell him you will pay for the damages." There went my savings. I'd probably have to enter indentured slavery before I could pay it off. "I have to finish things up here and then go file the report. After that I'll be home." And I'd be history. "Then we can sit down and talk this whole thing out."

Translation, he would tan my hide. I doubted that sitting down would be on my list of activities in the near future. "Now get going." He gave me a swat. "I want to get this finished up as soon as possible."

After I apologized to Mr. Pickford and promised to pay for the damages, I started off across the field. This had to be the worst trouble I'd been in, in my life. I heard the pounding of running feet coming close behind me.

"Katie! Wait up." I stopped to let Tim catch up with me. "So what's the verdict? I saw your dad with you."

Who hadn't? "I probably won't be able to do anything for awhile. He's pretty upset." The biggest understatement of the summer. "I'm supposed to go straight home and wait for him. Why do we always get caught?"

Tim shrugged. "We just have that kind of luck, I guess. Is your dad going to file a report?"

I nodded. "He has to. Destruction of property is pretty heavy duty, even for us."

Timmy slouched down. "My old man's gonna love this one. He'll hit the roof, but the only thing he'll really care about is who is going to pay for it."

"Tell him not to worry. I've already been instructed that it's coming out of my pocket." I glanced around. "Look, I've got to get going or my dad will give me an extra ration for disobedience." One of his watchwords. "I'll give you a call when I can."

When I got home, I took off my shoes before going in the house. My clothes had soot all over them. I decided to take a shower before Daddy came home. I grabbed a change of clothes and went into the bathroom. I not only had soot streaked across my face, but it darkened my blonde hair too.

It felt so good to get in the shower and to just let the hot water run over my body. Washing my hair, I started to relax for the first time since the fire broke out. "Oh, no!" My head jerked up. "The flask." It was still in the shed. There was no way my Daddy was going to overlook it. I definitely had more trouble than I bargained for. I quickly finished my shower.

I had to think of a way out of this one. Daddy would either ground me for the next four years or send me off to boarding school. I couldn't cope with either alternative. Glancing at the clock, I realized it wouldn't be much longer before he got home. I didn't have much time.

A tiny voice at the back of my brain told me to take off. Not forever. Just until his anger had a chance to cool a little. Grabbing my knapsack from the hall closet, I ran to my room. I didn't have any time to waste. If I stuck around too long, I wouldn't have a good enough head start. That was my mistake the last time I ran off, and I didn't want to repeat it.

After throwing a few clothes and some food in the bag, I took my money out of the shoe box in the closet and ran out the door. The town was so small that it didn't take long to come to the edge. Flat, open country surrounded the town for miles, and it contained no place to hide. If I stuck close to the road, I would be caught for sure. I had to cross the whole territory before Daddy started looking for me.

After running for an hour, my side ached, and my lungs burned with every breath. Each step felt like it would be my last, but I knew I had to keep going. I couldn't afford to slow down because I was still a long way from any hope of a hiding place. The sun sank in the sky which happened to be the only thing in my favor at the moment.

Half an hour later, the sun was down and twilight deepened. The heat of the day cooled. I slowed to a walk, not able to run any longer. Marathons would never be my strong point. I'd covered a lot of distance though, and that gave me a good feeling inside. If I could just make it to another town, it didn't matter where it was.

An uneasy feeling made me turn around. I could see the far off beam of a flashlight. It could only be my Daddy. I fell to the ground and lay as still as I could. Hopefully the grass would be tall enough to hide me. If I ran, he would see the movement and catch me in minutes. My heart raced and it was difficult to breathe softly. The dry grass had an almost hay-like smell and it made me feel like sneezing.

A footstep sounded to my left. Holding my breath, I closed my eyes hoping against hope that Daddy would pass by. The beam of the flashlight on my face shattered that hope.

"Get up, Katie." He put his hand out to help me up. "Let's go home."

No yelling? No lecture? I must be in worse trouble than even I imagined. If Daddy were talking, I knew he would at least be blowing off some steam. We walked back to where he parked the car and he drove us home in silence.

"Daddy?"

He held up his hand. "Wait until we get back to the house." Great. Suffer in silence. He must be furious. When we pulled into the drive, the car barely stopped before I got out and ran into the house.

"Katie, please come out here."

I stuck my hands in my pockets and slowly walked into the living room. "I thought you would have wanted me in my room." That's where punishment usually got dealt out.

"Sit down, please. We have a lot to talk about."

Dumbfounded, I sat on the couch. "You don't want me to get the helper?" I couldn't believe this.

He shook his head. "We don't need it."

"What happened to 'spare the rod and spoil the child'?" The words dripped with sarcasm. "Or are you finally admitting that I'm too old to be spanked?" I knew I was getting myself in deeper, but I couldn't stop myself. "Or maybe I'm just not deserving enough this time."

"Stop." The word burst from him with anguish. Uh-oh, I may have pushed him too far. It was almost like I was asking to be punished, and that was crazy. "I've been thinking a lot about you lately, and what's best for you." That didn't sound very good for me. "I've done the best I could." He sat down in his leather armchair. "But, I don't think it's enough anymore." Pain clouded his blue eyes, and it made me feel terrible, worse than any spanking. "You must think that too, otherwise you wouldn't have run off."

"Daddy, it's not you." How could he think that? "I don't know what's wrong with me lately." That was true enough. "But, I'm the problem."

"Why did you run off?" He put the question very quietly.

To avoid some hassle. "I don't know." Daddy waited for me to continue. "I knew you were angry, and I just didn't want to deal with it." I swallowed hard. "I was going to come back after you cooled down some."

His head bowed. "I wanted us always to be able to talk things out. But if you're afraid of me. . ." His voice trailed off as he couldn't continue.

"I'm not afraid of you, Daddy. I left because I knew I was wrong." And I didn't feel like paying for the consequences of my actions. "That and I feel so restless sometimes, that I just don't know what to do."

Daddy looked back up at me. "In other words, you're restless because you're not happy at home."

"That's not it. It's this God forsaken hole of a place we live in."

Daddy's face looked like a thunder-cloud for a minute. "I don't like to hear you talk that way."

My eyes couldn't meet his glare. "I'm sorry, Daddy." I looked at my shoes, and my cheeks burned a little. "I just don't want to live here for the rest of my life." I felt like I was under a microscope in this town. "Here, the biggest news of the week is which way the wind is blowing the fumes from the Farley's outhouse." I stood up. "I know you like it here, but I want to see what the world has to offer." I started to pace. "This place is so close, with everybody knowing everybody else's business, that I feel like I can't breathe sometimes." My breath came harder and faster because just the thought of the town made me feel claustrophobic.

"That's one of the reasons I'm sending you to live with your Uncle Charley."

"What!" Stopping in my tracks, my mouth dropped open, I couldn't believe my ears. I didn't want to be sent away.

"You need to be looked after a little better."

"Don't tell me you've been listening to those idiots who think you don't take care of me very well."

"Now just calm down a minute."

I guess I got a little excited. Some people thought that Daddy should leave his office of sheriff to look after me better, just because I got into mischief from time to time.

Daddy stared straight into my eyes with a serious look on his face. "While you know for the most part I don't agree with them, lately I'm beginning to think that they may have a point. Let's take this afternoon as a prime example. Accidentally burning down a shed because you're experimenting with cigarettes and alcohol might make some people argue that you need a little firmer parental control." I sat back down on the couch feeling as if I had been hit in the stomach. "Yes, I found the flask. Katie, I just don't know what to do with you anymore." He stood up and began rubbing his forehead again. "I tried to raise you with a good, upright background and you seem to be rejecting everything I ever taught you." He bit his lip. "Maybe in a different atmosphere you can straighten back out."

I felt like crying. "I'll straighten out. You don't have to send me away."

He shook his head. "There are just things that I can't give you. And I'm not talking about material things." He was really serious. "My little girl is growing up, and I think you need a woman around. If your Mamma was still alive, things would be different." His voice got kind of choky sounding, the way it did whenever he talked about Mamma. She died in a car accident when I was a baby. A drunk driver hit her and she died from the impact. That's when my Daddy moved us to this little town in the middle of nowhere.

"Daddy? I thought Aunt Libby died in the same accident as Mamma."

Daddy's face went blank, and his eyes had a frozen look about them. "She did." Daddy really didn't like talking about Mamma's death.

"Did Uncle Charley get remarried?"

"No. My brother John's girl, Sarah, lives there. In fact, she's been living there a number of years now." Good for her. "I think she'll be a good influence on you."

How could he know that? As far as I knew, he hadn't visited his brother for years. "But Daddy, I don't want to go. Let me stay here. I'll behave myself. I give you my word."

"You sure changed your mind in a hurry. An hour ago you were running away. You couldn't wait to get out of this place."

I stood up and walked over to the picture of Daddy and me that stood there. Daddy had me on his back for the piggy-back race, my cheek laid next to his, both smiling and happy because we won the race. "That's different." My voice had an edge to it, a harshness, because I felt like crying, and didn't want to. Crying meant weakness, and I didn't want to be weak in front of my Daddy.

I took a slow deep breath. "I wanted to leave here, but I didn't want to be sent away." My finger traced the frame of the picture. "I just wanted to be gone for a few days, a week at the most, and give you a chance to cool down some." Continuing to rub the picture frame, I felt my control become firmer. "I knew that you wouldn't like me trying smoking. But everything I've known firsthand has been in this town, and it all amounts to nothing." I turned back to face Daddy. "I want to experience life. I feel like it's passing me by here."

"There's time enough for that." That's what he always said. I just didn't want to wait. "And there are smarter things to do."

I knew he would get around to that. "There wasn't anything to do, and I wanted to try something different."

Daddy frowned. "Boredom does not excuse your actions. You have a good brain in that head of yours, and lately you've been acting without using it."

My fingers started tapping the edge of the couch. "I never said that boredom was an excuse." I hated when he put words into my mouth. "And I did use my brain."

"Really? Let's take a look at the results."

"I know what happened." I was having difficulty controlling my anger. "I didn't think I would burn the shed down. It was an accident."

He pointed his finger at me. "That's exactly what I'm getting at. You're not thinking through the consequences of your actions." To emphasize his point, he slapped the back of one hand on to his outstretched palm. "You are a McCabe and you have got to start acting like one. For once, take responsibility for your actions upon yourself. I can't do it for you."

That did it. "I never asked to be a McCabe and I wish to God I was never born one." Life certainly would have been easier. "It's not fair that I have to be a certain way just because of my last name." I wanted to hurt Daddy and I knew that this would. "Someone up there screwed up when they sent me to this family, because I don't belong."

"That's enough Katherine." Daddy spoke softly, but I could tell by the tone in his voice that I'd better stop.

"Daddy, I'm trying to make you understand something. The McCabe's have a reputation that I didn't have anything to do with." And I didn't want any part of it either. "I'm never allowed to just be Katie. No matter what I do, I'm measured by a standard that I can't live up to."

McCabes stood tall, did the right thing, helped others in need before thinking of themselves, and were kind, gentle, moral, and spiritual leaders wherever they went. I looked at the floor. "Maybe that's why I seem to go out of my way to get into trouble. I want to be known for myself, not some family that I don't even know." The McCabe reputation stretched for miles. Even in my town folks knew of it. I don't think the reputation would have been quite so strong or widespread if my grandparents hadn't had seven boys, all of whom went out of their way to prove the McCabe reputation true.

"Daddy, I don't want to leave you." I loved him too much. "I'll even try to be like a McCabe if it will make you love me enough to keep me here."

Daddy's eyes softened and a tremor ran across his cheek. Then, he reached out, took my hand gently in his, and pulled me closer to him. "Katie, sweetheart, it's because I love you so much that I want you to go live with your Uncle Charley."

Tears welled up in my eyes. "I can't believe you don't want me anymore."

Hugging me close, he stroked my hair. "I do want you. This has been the hardest decision I've ever had to make." After holding me tight for a moment he continued. "There is another reason for my decision, and I need you to listen because it is difficult enough for me to say." He took a deep breath. "I haven't been feeling well, and when I went to the doctor, he thinks I'm very sick and needs to put me through a bunch of tests. I'll have to spend some time in the hospital and need someone to look after you while I'm going through all of this, because I won't be able to. Please trust me; this is the best for you."

I pulled my head back to look into his eyes. "But if you're sick, then I should be with you to take care of you." He gently shook his head. The tears spilled over, and I buried my head in his chest. "Couldn't I just go for a visit instead then, until you are better?"

"No, a visit won't do. School starts next week, and I want you to be enrolled there." I pulled away from Daddy and flopped back onto the couch. "Sulking won't do you any good. Your Uncle Charley suggested that you go live with him over a month ago. He thought it would be a good idea for you to get settled in before school started, but

I didn't want to let go of you yet."

"You knew for over a month that you were going to send me away, and you're just telling me now?" That might even be the worst hurt of all.

"I was thinking about it before I went to the doctor, but didn't make my decision until I got some of the results back and have been trying to figure things out." He brushed my bangs back from my eyes. "Your Uncle suggested the move when I was trying to figure out how to handle how wild you have been getting, but I didn't want to prolong the pain of separation. And if I was going to take Charley up on his suggestion, I wanted you to have a good summer without this move hanging over your head."

We argued back and forth. Or I should say, I argued and Daddy stayed calm, but didn't budge an inch. Finally, he told me I'd better pack because I was going, whether he had to put me on the bus kicking and screaming, or not. When Daddy got that certain tone in his voice, and his jaw looked like it had been carved in granite, I knew it was useless to argue because he meant what he said.

My packing consisted of throwing my clothes into an old battered suitcase. I looked around and tried to decide if I needed to take anything else. In my room, I had very few things, and an overabundance of one. Books. My bookcase bulged with them. I put shelves on the walls just to hold them, and even then they overflowed. I had to take some books with me, in case Uncle Charley didn't have any I liked. I quickly pulled five favorites off the shelf, put them in the suitcase, and closed the lid.

I stomped into the next room dragging my suitcase behind. I never thought of myself as sentimental, but looking around the room brought a lump to my throat. The worn, faded couch where Daddy and I had spent many hours together, the fireplace that had toasted bag after bag of marshmallows, the plaques on the wall that my Daddy earned from the town. Everything worn, perhaps a little shabby, nothing new or shiny, but homey and loved.

My eyes stopped when they came to Daddy's face. His face looked gray and old, and a shock ran through my body. Had I done that to him? Was it his illness? Why hadn't I noticed it sooner? When younger, I used to think that God must look exactly like my Daddy; big, tall, blonde, with a twinkle in his blue eyes, and a smile on his face. His very presence seemed to make trouble disappear. My Daddy could do any and everything. My Daddy was my hero, stronger than Hercules, mightier than Superman, yet more gentle and kind than all the super-heroes put together. In my eyes, Greek mythological gods lacked sparkle when compared with my Daddy.

By the time I finished packing, it was time to leave for the bus station. The sky grew misty gray with the arrival of dawn. When Daddy drove me to the bus station, the silence between us hung as heavy as a steel anchor. Neither one of us said anything until the bus rolled in. Daddy broke the silence first.

"Do you have everything?" I nodded. "Here's your ticket." He held it out to me. "Have Uncle Charley give me a call when you get there." The bus horn honked. "I guess this is good-bye for now. Be good. I'll come to see you as soon as all my tests are done, to see how you're doing." He hugged me tight.

I twisted out of his grasp, grabbed my bag and stalked on to the bus without a word. I wanted to throw myself into his arms and not let go. I wanted him to tell me that everything was going to be okay, but he couldn't. The longer I would have waited, the harder it would have been to go, and my throat was so constricted I couldn't speak. Besides, I was really angry. And scared. I didn't know it was possible to have so many emotions flooding through me at the same time.

As soon as I found my seat, the bus pulled out of the station. Looking out my window, I watched my Daddy until he became a tiny speck on the horizon. The bus rattled and bumped its way down the road, the seats creaked, and the sides seemed to groan more with every mile. The windows didn't stay shut, so my mouth felt as dry as cotton from the dust that poured in, and the heat of the day made the bus feel like the inside of an oven. I felt cranky from lack of sleep, and my eyes felt gritty and burned from the dust.

At least I had the seat to myself, and could sit through the long ride without someone interrupting my thoughts. What a sight I must be for the other passengers, my arms folded across my chest, a scowl for an expression, and my long, blonde hair hanging in my face. I crouched down low in the seat and thrust my knees against the back of the seat in front of me. I didn't want to make this trip, and didn't care what anyone else thought about me either. How could Daddy send me away from him, especially when he was sick? What if he didn't get better? I had to push that thought out of my mind. I didn't even want to think about that possibility. He had to get better, he just had to. The motion of the bus, along with my sleepless night, soon lulled me to sleep.

Down on the Farm

T he bus hit a big rut in the road and bounced me into wakefulness. My head ached and I couldn't get the argument Daddy and I had out of my mind. I needed to be thinking about what was up ahead and quit dwelling on the past. All I knew about Uncle Charley, his two sons Matthew and Mark, and Sarah was from the stories my Daddy had told me. That and they bore the name of McCabe, which meant they probably upheld the McCabe reputation. Here I was, with every bump getting closer to the home of the McCabe boys. I wished sometimes that I could change my name so people would accept me for who I am, instead of trying to force me into the McCabe mold.

The bus finally rolled to a stop at a station, if it could be called that. A flat wooden bench set in the dirt to the side of the road. Before the bus came to a complete stop, I stood up, grabbed my bag from the overhead, and walked to the front. The door hardly had a chance to open, when a man hopped on board.

"Katie McCabe?" I nodded and brushed my hair out of my eyes. "I'm your cousin Matthew." He grinned, and I stood at the top of the stairs frozen to the spot, absolutely speechless. My cousin Matthew looked exactly like my Daddy in some of the pictures I had seen of him as a young man. I don't know what I expected. Some weak little guy I guess, but not someone so big or good-looking.

"Well, don't just stand there, we don't have all day. And I'm sure the driver wants to get on with his trip too." He reached up. "Here, let me help you." As he lifted me off the bus, I noticed how wonderfully his muscles flexed. He definitely wasn't weak. "If you have all your things, I'll take you out to the farm, and then I have to get back to work."

"Farm? My Daddy didn't tell me it was a farm."

Matthew tossed my suitcase into the trunk, and slammed the lid. "It's just a small one, but Dad likes to work on it in his spare time. We all help out too. Sarah's out there right now waiting for you. She'll help you get settled in. And in a couple hours Mark, Dad, and I will be back." We got into the car and Matthew guided it away from the open air station and onto the road.

"The farm doesn't happen to be in the middle of town does it?" I felt let down. Since I had to come, I at least wanted to be in town, where something might happen.

"No, the farm isn't in town, thank goodness. We're not too far from it though. Close enough I'd say."

I turned and looked out the window. Hills of deep green and contrasting gray-green stood all around, covered with beautiful trees. The sunlight shining down hit an occasional meandering brook, and it sparkled like a river of jewels. All the scenery looked like it belonged in a painting.

Matthew spoke again, after a little while, almost like he read my thoughts. "It sure is beautiful isn't it? It kind of makes you feel peaceful, at least it does me. I guess that's why I like living out here, instead of around so many buildings." He turned the car off the road onto a little lane. Rounding a curve, I could see the house. "Well, here we are. Welcome to the McCabe farm." A nice, cheery looking place, white with blue trim and a long wooden porch, and a porch swing to go with it.

As we drove up, a beautiful girl came out of the front door. She wore a simple peasant style blouse and skirt, and moved with grace and ease. All of a sudden, I felt clumsy and not put together quite right. I reluctantly stepped out of the car and walked toward the house. Matthew grabbed my bag, and passed me by with his long stride. As I followed him, it hit me forcibly that I didn't want to be here at all.

"The bus was a little late, so I grabbed Katie and we came straight here." Matthew turned his head toward me. "Sarah'll be able to show you where everything is."

I didn't want to know where everything was. As I came up to the door, Sarah gave me big hug of welcome. "I'm so glad you've come to live with us, Katie, I could hardly wait for you to get here."

I knew the time for battle had come. If I didn't want to stay here, I would have to be as awful as possible, so they'd send me back home. I strove to make my voice icy and rude. "First of all, you can stop being so sickeningly sweet. The only reason I am here is by force. I hate this place, I don't want to be here, and I wish to God I had never laid eyes on you." Then I brushed past her on into the house, but not before I caught the look of dismay she exchanged with Matthew. As I walked into the house, I had a smile on my face and a sense of triumph in my heart. I knew I had scored.

Sarah followed me into the house. "Matt had to get back to work. Grab your bag, and I'll show you to our room."

"Our room? Does this mean I actually have to share a room with you?"

Sarah seemed determined to ignore the bite of my words. "Oh, don't worry; it's a pretty good-sized room."

I looked straight into her big, green eyes. "It's not the size of the room that bothers me. It's the roommate I have to share it with." Sarah pressed her lips tightly together and looked away, and I knew I had scored again. If I could keep up the rude comments, I knew I could really get under her skin. We walked through the door and into the room. I put an expression on my face like I had tasted something awful. "I can't live in this room."

Suspicion sprang into Sarah's eyes as she turned toward me. "Why not?"

I looked around as if trying to find the precise words to sum it up. "It's so prissy-looking, I could vomit." Actually it looked very nice. Dainty flowered wallpaper and matching bedspreads, a vase of flowers on the chest of drawers, frilly white curtains at the window, and everything spic and span clean.

"Well, get used to it. You can't very well share a room with the boys, and besides Uncle Charley's, this is the only other bedroom."

I narrowed my eyes and drew out my words to give them punch.

"I'd rather sleep in a barn."

She raised one eyebrow as her eyes sparked. "That can be arranged." I forgot that when you lived on a farm, you couldn't offer to sleep in the barn unless you were serious. By the tone of her voice, I knew I was skating on very thin ice. "The bed in the corner is yours, the right half of the closet, and the middle two drawers of the dresser."

I put my suitcase on my bed and opened it up. I didn't want to unpack, to put my things in this strange bedroom. It seemed too sudden, too fast for me to be here, with everything ready for me. Unpacking would make it real. I would have to face that Daddy really was sick, too sick to take care of me. "How long have you known I was coming?" That small, vulnerable sounding voice didn't even seem like mine.

"Uncle Charley told us that you would be coming over a month ago, but he wasn't sure of the exact date. A few days ago he told us you would arrive today. We've been anxiously waiting ever since." Sarah came up behind me and put a sympathetic hand on my shoulder.

Glancing at the contents of my suitcase, I felt inadequate again. I twitched my shoulder and turned to look her straight in the eyes. "After all that anticipation, I must be a major disappointment." Sarah opened her mouth as if to say something. "If you say otherwise, you're either a hypocrite or a fool." I was getting pretty good at being snotty. She quickly clamped her mouth shut, and narrowed her eyes. "What did Uncle Charley tell you about me? And what reasons did he give for me to come live here?" Part of me didn't want the answer that my tone demanded. I didn't want to hear that my Daddy was too sick. I didn't want to hear that he didn't want me anymore.

Sarah hesitated and took a deep breath. "I don't think it's my place to say anything. You should talk to Uncle Charley about that. If you really want to know."

"What a cop out. I hate people who play it safe." Why couldn't she tell me anyway? "I can guess what some of it was at least. I'm always in trouble and my Daddy couldn't handle me, so I had to be sent away." I raked my bangs out of my face. "They decided I needed a motherly touch, and you're it. What a laugh that is. I wouldn't listen to you if you were my grandmother, let alone just a cousin."

Sarah pulled her head back and blinked her eyes as if I tried to hit her. "That's enough." Then her lips tightened, and anger sparked again in her eyes. It made them look like flashing emeralds. "You need to get a grip on yourself and shape up if you want to live here."

I turned back to the bed and dumped the contents of my suitcase out. "That's my point, Sarah. I don't want to live here." I slammed the suitcase closed and slid it under the bed, then turned to face her again.

"You say you've known about my coming here for over a month. Well, I just found out about the move last night. I was forced to come and I don't want to be here."

"Since you are here, Katie, I suggest you make the best of it. If you have any questions, I'll be in the kitchen fixing supper. As soon as you finish unpacking, I will expect your help."

With that, Sarah spun on her heel and strode out of the room. My pile of clothes looked pretty pathetic heaped on the bed. Opening my side of the closet, I noticed that Sarah had even stocked it with padded hangers, something I'd never had before. I hung up the one dress I brought with me. I had more dresses, but at home there seemed to be no reason to wear them, and I just didn't think to bring the rest of them along. The dress looked silly hanging there alone, so I grabbed my shirts and put them in the closet too. It took very little time to put everything away, so I went out to the kitchen, as commanded.

Against the sunny yellow background of the kitchen stood Sarah, looking prettier than ever, if that were possible. Her long, wavy, chestnut locks had been pulled back into a loose ponytail, and tied with a cream colored scarf. Intent on stirring something in a pan, head slightly bent forward, her long, thick, dark lashes almost rested on her cheeks, which were creamy in complexion, but somewhat flushed from the steam. My stomach grumbled in protest as I caught a whiff of steak being cooked. It smelled so good, I could almost taste it.

At the sound of my stomach, Sarah looked up and gave me a big friendly smile. It would be harder than I first thought to be mean to her. When someone showed they had true sweetness in them, like Sarah, it seemed more difficult to do something rotten to them. That is something that no one would ever accuse me of having, true sweetness.

"You're just in time to help me out. Everything is almost ready, and Uncle Charley and the boys should be home any minute." A quick frown crossed her face as she continued to look at me. "We need to get your hair out of the way before you start. I've got another scarf. Come here, and I'll tie your hair back like mine." After tying the scarf in my hair, she turned me around to take another look, and smiled. "Much better. Now, there's lettuce, celery, and carrots in the vegetable drawer, if you could make a salad I'd sure appreciate it. After that, the table needs to be set, and then we should be able to eat."

I certainly needed to hear that. Starving didn't quite capture how hungry I felt, and the smells from the cooking food drove me nearly crazy. I hadn't eaten since the day before because I was running through a field at dinnertime, too angry to eat breakfast, and too forgetful to remember to pack a lunch for the trip. My insides were hollow.

"Hurry up now. I got started a little late, so I'm behind." At least she didn't say I was the reason for the lateness. She probably thought it though.

I opened the refrigerator door, hunted around a bit, and took out the vegetables. "So what happens if it goes on the table a couple of minutes late? Does Uncle Charley turn into a beast and throw you out of the house?"

"No, Uncle Charley would never say a word if supper were late." I started to pull the lettuce apart. "Remember to wash the vegetables first." My lip curled up at the words. What did she think I would do, roll them on the ground first? Oh well, if that's what she wanted to think. I shrugged and turned on the tap.

Sarah kept rattling on about Uncle Charley. "He's a good, sweet man. The best kind there is. That's why I like everything to be just the way he likes it." How sickening. I tore apart the lettuce and tossed it into a bowl. I grabbed the carrots and began to cut them up. When I finished, I realized I had chopped them into hunks instead of slicing them. That meant I had to take the time to re-cut them.

"Will you please set the table now? I hear the cars at the end of the lane. I'll finish the salad." She said it nicely enough, but it felt like a put down because I hadn't finished. After opening a few cupboards, I managed to find the plates and glasses. As I put the plates on the table, the stoneware banged and sounded like it might break. "Take it easy with those plates."

"I didn't mean to put them down so hard." I couldn't do anything without her saying something about it.

"All right. Just be a little more careful."

We worked in silence as I put the plates around the table. I heard boots shuffling on the porch. The door opened, and in walked a tall, lean man. He had dark brown hair, almost black, with a touch of gray at the sides. Even in his work clothes of blue jeans and a plaid shirt, he looked like a man of importance. Uncle Charley owned a construction company, and Matt and Mark worked for him. Daddy had at least told me that much.

"You must be Katie." His voice sounded deep and strong, like Daddy's, the kind of voice that gave comfort because it was solid and couldn't be shaken.

I wanted to try and shake that calm though, so I tried a smart answer. "Good guess."

"I trust Sarah got you settled in all right."

Well, my first try fell flat. I knew if my plan was to work, I would really have to get to Uncle Charley, because he would make the final decision. "Oh yes. I'm all unpacked. My question is when do I get to pack up again?"

A trace of confusion crossed Uncle Charley's face. "Pack up? Why?"

"I'm going back home. You don't think I'm going to stay here for very long do you?" I swiped at my bangs to get them out of my eyes, and my voice got a little louder as I continued. "This is just temporary. You'll see. My Daddy will be calling for me to come home as soon as his tests are all done. He'll be too lonely without me."

I spoke with a lot more confidence than I felt. Daddy didn't often change his mind about things, and he seemed to want me to at least stay through the school year. A troubled expression replaced the confusion on Uncle Charley's face, and that gave me a sense of satisfaction. "We'll talk a little later about this. Right now though, I need to wash for supper."

I didn't get as much of a reaction as I wanted. I heard some stomping outside on the porch. The door opened and in walked Matthew, and right behind him another big, tall, handsome, hunk of a guy. Only Mark had dark hair and eyes, and dimples in his cheeks. Where Matthew looked like my Daddy, Mark looked like his. Maybe I shouldn't be so hasty about wanting to leave. If all the guys around here looked like my cousins, my eyes'd be in hog heaven. The only guy I hung around with at home was Timmy Lawrence, because he could forget my Daddy's office of sheriff, and my last name of McCabe. Besides which he was about the only guy around even close to my age and my closest pal.

"Hey Sarah, is supper ready? I'm so hungry I could eat the hide off a horse."

"Get yourself washed up, Mark, and it'll be on the table. Katie, will you please help me carry things over?"

I realized I was just standing there, fork in hand, not even moving. Mark strode out of the room, and I found my eyes following his every move until he disappeared from view. He hadn't noticed me, or didn't show that he knew I was there, and I felt strangely let down. I wanted him to notice me. Both he and Matthew were so handsome, that I wanted their attention.

I went into the kitchen in somewhat of a daze. "Sarah? Are all the guys around here as good-looking as those cousins of ours?"

Sarah gave a short laugh, and amusement put a twinkle in her eyes. "No, Matt and Mark are kind of special, although, we do have some very nice-looking guys in the area." Her smile widened and her right eyebrow rose as she teased me. "Changing your mind about wanting to leave?"

"Well, I might think about sticking around for awhile, with the right type of bait of course."

"Oh, of course. Nothing but the best." We carried the last dish to the table. Sarah patted my shoulder and gave me a quick squeeze.

Footsteps sounded as Uncle Charley came into the room. "Are we ready to sit down to the table?"

Sarah nodded, and then called toward the hall. "Come on, Mark. It'll be cold if you wait much longer."

He came in and we all sat down with Mark sitting directly across from me. He had to notice me now. Matt smiled at me as he sat down and my heart did another flip. I had to tear my mind away from thoughts of my cousins and remember my plans for being sent back home just as soon as Daddy was well enough. I had to make myself as unpleasant as possible, so that I quickly became the unwanted guest. If Uncle Charley were anything like Daddy, he'd flip if I started eating before the meal was blessed. I deliberately started dishing food onto my plate, and took a bite.

"Hold on there little miss. We haven't given our thanks to the Lord yet. At this table, you don't touch the food until that has been done. Is that understood?"

I stared down at my plate and I felt the back of my neck flush. "Yes, sir." While Uncle Charley said grace, I scolded myself for reacting like a child caught with her hand in the cookie jar. After all, I had done it on purpose. But, I didn't want Matt and Mark to think poorly of me. I didn't know why, but I wanted their approval. I had to set that thought aside though. I wanted to go home.

As soon as the prayer ended, Mark grabbed the salad from in front of him. "Hey, is this some sort of new-fangled salad? I've never heard of one with carrot chunks before." Instead of just the back of my neck, I could feel my whole face turning beet red.

"Is it all right to eat now?" I intentionally made my voice sound as snotty as possible. It helped cover my embarrassment as well as being generally irritating. As I glanced up I caught Mark's eye, and he looked like he might laugh.

Uncle Charley answered me in a dry sounding voice. "Yes. I'm frankly surprised Sam didn't teach you better table manners. He knows what is expected at the table and I thought he would have taught you the same."

My head snapped around to glare into his brown eyes. "Yeah? How do you know my Daddy didn't bring me up in the holier-than-thou McCabe tradition?" I was flaming mad.

"By your actions."

That made me furious. Why attack Daddy for something I did. "You're wrong!" I could feel the heat of my anger burning in my throat. "Daddy taught me a lot of things, including how to behave. He'd have tanned my hide for the way I've acted today, but you wouldn't know about that, would you?"

The lack of sleep and food hit me suddenly and I felt my control slipping away. My voice had risen and I tried desperately to calm myself down again. "I decided on my own not to do things the McCabe way anymore. It has nothing to do with Daddy. So don't you. . ." I lost control completely and ended up shouting. ". . .don't any of you ever say anything against my Daddy again."

Uncle Charley frowned and slowly put down his fork. "Katie, you either settle yourself down and apologize for your behavior, or you may leave the table." He spoke calmly, but his voice had the same rock solid tone that my Daddy had when he wasn't going to stand for any more. "I don't allow shouting at supper, or any other time."

I stood up abruptly, knocking my chair over, but paused before I answered. I didn't want to shout again because I wanted to be in control. Or at least seem to be. "I won't apologize, and I don't care what you don't allow at your table, or in your house."

I saw a quick angry look flit across Uncle Charley's mouth. "Then you may be excused to go to your room."

I thought about making a dash for the front door, but decided against it. Matt or Mark would probably catch me before I got off the porch. It would embarrass me to have them haul me back inside and I had already embarrassed myself enough for one meal. Besides, once outside, I wouldn't know where to go. "At least in my room I'll have better company." I ran into my room. On the way, I could hear Mark give a hoot of laughter.

"It looks like Uncle Sam raised a little hell-cat."

I slammed the door to drown out any reply. I was sure I would be the main topic of dinner conversation. As I sat there on the bed, I began to think about home. At home, when things like this happened, I could always run and find Timmy Lawrence. Timmy and I would go down by the river bank and talk for hours. He listened and really seemed to understand. Then he would say something to make me feel better.

The town labeled Timmy an outcast. The town biddies frequently felt it their duty to tell Daddy he shouldn't allow me to associate, as they put it, with Timmy. His father wasn't the right type, and therefore a bad influence on both of us. In the town's eyes, Timmy led me astray. If they turned it around, they would have been more accurate. Daddy never paid any attention to what they had to say and he told me that if they didn't bother to get to know Timmy before saying anything about him or his father, then what they said had no value anyway.

Thinking about Timmy made me remember the fun we had getting into trouble. Like the time I found some powder that made Mrs. Simpson, our teacher at the time, sneeze. We put a lot of it in the tray of the chalkboard. It looked just like chalk dust. Every time Mrs. Simpson got near the board to give us some problems to work on, she had a sneezing attack and couldn't continue. She finally decided to go on with it even if she did start sneezing again. Timmy and I were in such hysterics by the time she was through, that she knew we had something to do with her mysterious sneezing fits.

We got immediate passes to the Principal's office and had to confess. Daddy came and got me, and I couldn't sit down again comfortably for two days after that. Timmy just got talked to by the Principal. That was it, but I think he suffered more than I did. He didn't like having a bad reputation and I thrived on making one. We got caught a lot. Even when we didn't get caught, Daddy would ask me about something that happened, and I couldn't lie to him. He always knew when I was involved somehow.

I wished Timmy had been able to come with me because I missed him and needed to talk to him. Daddy understood me pretty well too. He never backed down an inch from his expectations of me. But, he'd take me in his arms, and my troubles would disappear because he loved me, and nothing else mattered. I suddenly felt all alone and scared. I wanted to be at home so my Daddy could hug me and tell me tomorrow would be a better day.

Brooding about home would not help matters any. I knew Daddy wanted me to give this a try. As the bus pulled away from the station he looked smaller, almost shrunken, and tears were streaming down his face. I knew he missed me as much as I missed him. I would ask Uncle Charley to let me give him a call, except I figured he wouldn't let me, at least tonight. Maybe I should try to do well and fit in for Daddy's sake. He always wanted me to have the best. Maybe this was the only way for him to make sure I would get it. Didn't he know that the best for me was being with him?

Lost in thought, I didn't notice Sarah come in until she quietly sat down beside me. "I was going to bring you some supper since you didn't have a chance to eat any, but Uncle Charley said you missed out for tonight." She put a paper towel with something warm wrapped in it in my hand. "I brought you a biscuit anyway, because I know you haven't had anything since early this morning."

My stomach gurgled loudly as I smelled the biscuit. I quickly unwrapped it and brought it up to my mouth, but then stopped. I wanted to take it, but somehow felt I couldn't. I lowered it to my lap. I'm the one who had blown it. And I did it on purpose. I really didn't deserve for someone to be kind to me like this. I took one last sniff and handed it back to Sarah. "Thanks, but I don't want it." My stomach chose that moment to grumble really loud.

Concern passed across her face. "But you're hungry."

"Yeah. But I just don't feel right about eating it." A little respect crept into Sarah's eyes. Respect because I had some principles I stood on. "It was really nice of you to bring it though. I feel kind of bad about the way I acted earlier, and about the things I said to you."

She smiled. "That's all right. You're just hurting inside. Otherwise you'd never act that way. It's hard when you have to leave home." She stroked my hair and it gave me a sense of comfort. Things might not be as bad as I thought they'd be. "Now, Uncle Charley wants you to come and help me clear everything up. Then he wants you to get straight into bed and get a good nights sleep."

I heaved a big sigh. "I can use some sleep. I'm exhausted." When I did get into bed, my head barely touched the pillow before I fell asleep.

When I opened my eyes in the morning, I saw Sarah buzzing

around the room, dust cloth in hand humming as she worked. I didn't see how anyone could look so bright and cheerful so early in the morning. She smiled at me when she saw that I was awake.

"It's about time you woke up. The way you were sleeping, I thought you might be out until noon."

I pulled myself up to a sitting position. "I didn't sleep that long. What time is it anyway?"

"A couple of minutes before six. You'd better get up. We have a lot to do today."

I flopped back onto the pillow and pulled the covers over my face. "Six in the morning is not a time for any decent person to be getting up." I threw the blankets back and put my head up. "It's an hour made to be slept through. My brain doesn't even start until ten or eleven at the earliest."

She laughed. "Get used to it. You need to get moving now. There are eggs to be collected, breakfast to be made and cleared, and then we have to go into town."

When I didn't move, Sarah threw the dust cloth at me. I sat up and tossed it back. "So when's breakfast?" The hollow area that used to be called my stomach vaguely remembered food.

"You have to collect the eggs first. I think Mark is over at the barn right now. He'll be able to help you out a little."

My heart gave a leap at the thought of spending some time alone with my handsome cousin. Crazy though it may be, I had a crush on both of my male cousins. I couldn't do anything about it. I knew they would never feel the same way about me, but I couldn't help the way I felt. To them I was just a kid. The only way they'd think about me was as a cousin. I slowly got out from beneath the covers and got dressed. By the time I came back from the bathroom, Sarah had made my bed.

"You didn't have to do that. I would have made it." I snapped at her because I felt put out that she'd done me a favor.

"I know. I just thought I'd save you a little time this morning." I didn't want to owe anyone anything. Not even something so small and insignificant. "Just don't expect it to happen everyday, because it won't. Now go on out to the barn and give Mark a hand."

I stepped out into the bright sunlight. The air had the sweet, musty smell of morning, and it felt cool against my skin. The barn looked like it belonged in a picture, with its cracked and peeling red paint, and warped and weathered boards against the blue summer sky. The hens clucked in their coop out past the barn. I figured I'd better check with Mark to see if there was anything I could help him with first.

My eyes took a moment to adjust to the dark as I walked into the barn. I could barely make out Mark's outline squatted down and leaning forward to milk the cow. As I took another step forward, a huge dog rose to its feet with a growl, and I stopped in my tracks.

Mark glanced up as I stopped and raised a hand in greeting. "It's all right, Günter. It's just our little spitfire, Kit-Kat."

Kit-Kat? As I remembered his comment last night as I stormed from the room, I could feel my face getting hot. I guess it could have been worse, he could have told Günter to attack instead of giving me a nickname.

"Why don't you grab that stool over there, and I'll teach you how to milk ol' Bossy here."

It seemed too nice of a morning to be spoiled by a know-it-all, so I didn't tell Mark I already knew how to milk a cow. The strength of his hands over mine reminded me of when my Daddy taught me how to milk a cow. Daddy believed in helping out your neighbors, so he used to send me over to help Mr. Pickford with the milking and feeding of his animals. Mr. Pickford kept a cow, a goat, and some hens, as well as a horse at his place, and he was getting too old to take care of them right. He told me if I did a good job in taking care of the animals for him, that one day he would give me the horse. The horse was a beauty, and I wanted one of my own, so I always made sure the animals were doing well. Burning down the shed probably ruined my chances for getting the horse though.

After we finished milking Bossy, Mark took me to the chicken coop, introduced me to the hens, and insisted on showing me how to collect the eggs. After that, he gave me a short tour of the barn, and promised to show me more later. The whole time we were out there, Günter never left Mark's side.

I went back to the house and helped Sarah fix breakfast, my

thoughts still on home. The moment I got a whiff of cooking food, my stomach let out a grumble that could doubtless be heard in the middle of town. The beast of hunger was suddenly let loose.

Startled, Sarah looked up from the range. "My goodness! I can tell you are really hungry." No kidding. Maybe it had something to do with the fact that I hadn't eaten for about two days. Fortunately, the food was ready in a few minutes.

Seeing Matt again at breakfast, I couldn't get over his likeness to my Daddy. He would have won my heart on that score alone, without taking into account how nice he seemed to be. But every time I looked at him, it made me miss Daddy more than ever. Before leaving for work, Uncle Charley stopped to talk to me. "Katie, I want you to mind Sarah while I'm gone. As far as I'm concerned, she's in charge while I'm not here." Great, all I needed was one more boss. "I'll see you when I get home." He placed his hand on the doorknob. "Maybe after we finish this part of the job, we can spend some time together and get to know one another better." With that he left.

As I helped Sarah clear the breakfast things, I began to wonder why she lived with Uncle Charley and not with her own family. I didn't like to ask straight out because I didn't want to pry. I didn't even know how long she had lived with Uncle Charley. I could ask about that at least. She might even tell me why. "Sarah? How long have you lived here?"

"Let me see, eleven years I think." Her forehead wrinkled as she concentrated on remembering. "That's right. I came here when I was twelve." She paused as if to say more, then pursed her lips and gave a slight shake of her head. "Why do you want to know?"

She didn't seem upset by the question, but I turned away and shrugged. I couldn't tell her I was just being nosy. "No reason."

"Be a sweetie and vacuum for me, it's in the hall closet."

While I vacuumed, Sarah dusted the cabinets and scrubbed the counters. After a while, since I couldn't hear over the noise, Sarah motioned for me to turn it off. "That's all for now. Go ahead and put that thing away. It's almost time for me to leave for work." She stopped for a moment and gazed critically at me. I looked down to see if I had spilled anything on my pink pants or my blouse, but I couldn't find any spots. "Before we go, I want to fix your hair."

So that was it. I never did anything to my hair except run a brush through it. I let it hang wild and free all day. "What are you going to do to it?" I couldn't keep the suspicious tone out of my voice.

"I just thought I might braid it."

That would be all right. I just didn't want anything prissy, like a bun. She did it differently than I thought she would. Instead of gathering it up into a ponytail first, she braided it straight down the middle of my head. When she finished, she looked at me and frowned, then grabbed a barstool from under the sideboard and brought it over. "You sit there. I'll be right back."

I didn't want to sit down. I walked over to the mantle. I couldn't believe how many pictures there were on it. Several of the pictures were old. Some of the uncles I had never met, grandparents that died before I was born, Matt and Mark as little boys. All kinds. In the middle, tucked behind some others was a picture of my Daddy and his brothers outside of their house. He must have been about six, the shortest of the bunch, and his front tooth was missing.

"Come over here and sit down."

I turned around and then stopped. Sarah had a pair of scissors in her hand. "What are those things for?"

"Your bangs are too long. I can't see your eyes, so I'm going to give them a little trim."

Oh no. Daddy and I had more arguments than I could count about my bangs being too long. I brushed them quickly back. "They're not too long; they just fell in my face for a minute."

"And that's where they stay most of the time. You need to sit down so I can cut them."

How could I get out of this? I hated the feel of cold scissors against my forehead. And the sound of them sent shivers up my spine. Plus, little hairs got into my eyes afterwards, and fell down my top and made me itch.

"I don't want them cut. I'm growing them out." It sounded dumb, but it was the only thing I could think of on the spur of the moment.

Sarah put the scissors down on the table and gazed at me in an unruffled manner. "All right. Let's get a barrette and clip them back. That way they won't fall in your face anymore."

"Barrette?" I practically squeaked. That would be awful. With barrettes my hair stood out from the side of my head and made me look funny. I didn't want to look like a little girl. Maybe I could let her trim them just a teeny tiny bit. I walked slowly over and sat down. "Only trim them as far as my eyebrows. I don't want them higher than that."

She giggled. "You looked like you were walking the plank just then." She combed the hair down over my eyes, and started to cut. I stood up abruptly. "Sit down or they'll end up crooked."

"But you're cutting them too high." I couldn't believe it. I sounded like a whiny brat. I'd never been a whiner before.

Sarah put her hand on my shoulder and pushed me back down on the stool. "Since I've started to cut, I have to finish. They'll end up fine."

She had a point. I couldn't go around with one cut taken out of them. "You cut them in the center on purpose. That way I have to let you cut them short or I'll look stupid."

"I can't finish until you settle down." It didn't matter how upset I was, I couldn't really argue about it anymore. "As soon as I'm finished, we'll go into town. I have to work this morning from nine to one. I work at the gift shop next to the Post Office." As she kept talking, the scissors mercilessly continued across my forehead cutting my hair. "It'll be all right for you to come with me, and it'll give you a chance to meet some new people. Then we'll run some errands before we come back here." She stood back to make sure she had cut my bangs straight.

"There." She smiled. "You sure are a pretty thing."

"Me? You're the one who's pretty." I blurted the words out before I could stop myself. Never in my dreams did I consider myself pretty. I didn't figure myself to be ugly, but certainly not beautiful. Sarah was beautiful, and when she smiled, it was like the whole room would light up and she was stunning. I was like ground hamburger next to her.

"Take a look and see for yourself."

I went over to look in the mirror above the mantle. When I caught a glimpse of myself, I couldn't believe the difference. Because Sarah was watching for my reaction, I made a face at the mirror. "Oh no." I put as much agony in the two words as I could. I had to get Sarah back for cutting my bangs shorter than I wanted and this was the best way I could think of. "I hope they grow back soon."

Actually, with my hair pulled back from my face instead of hiding it, I did almost look pretty. As I snuck another look in the mirror, my blue eyes sparkled back at me, and I felt that there might be a chance I had inherited some of the family's good looks.

"I can see I'm going to have to keep an eye on you with the boys. They'll be falling right and left over you." Sarah didn't seem at all upset that I didn't like what she had done. "Now, if you can pull yourself away from the mirror, we have to go or I'll be late." I had let her see right through me. So much for pretending I thought I looked awful.

It only took about ten minutes to get to town, and I liked that because I didn't want to be too far from it. If I could get a bicycle, I'd be able to get to and from town pretty easily and not have to rely on anybody's kindness or goodwill to get me there. I didn't like having to rely on anyone for anything. When we arrived at the shop, Sarah introduced me to her friend and boss, Mrs. Denton. Tall and lean, she had gray hair, grayish skin, and everything about her seemed drab and faded.

I felt uncomfortable being introduced because I didn't know what to say, or what was expected of me. So, after an awkward pause, I walked away and looked around the shop a little bit. Mrs. Denton soon went back to her office, and Sarah took out some books and started pricing things. It didn't take long to look at everything in the small shop. It had all sorts of knick-knacks, cups, stationery, and little gift items. I wanted to get out and see some things. I didn't want to stay inside any longer.

I walked over to the counter. "Is it all right if I go out and look around town?"

Sarah shook her head. "No. I don't want you to go out alone." She hadn't even looked up from her work.

I shoved my hands in my pockets. "Why not? I'm old enough to take care of myself." I just wanted to see what there was around this place. "I won't get lost or anything like that either."

She switched her attention from a figurine to a book, and flipped through some pages. "I'm sure you're old enough, but you don't know your way around. And I want to know where you are. That's final! No arguments."

I spun angrily around and stomped off muttering to myself. She just wanted to know what kind of mischief I might be in.

"What did you say?" Her voice had an edge to it that made me stop.

"Nothing." I had no problem making my voice as sullen and bad-tempered as possible. She was treating me like a baby, and it made me mad. At home I could have gone out instead of being cooped up inside for half the day. If I had known that I was going to be a prisoner, I'd have brought one of my books. I started walking toward the back of the shop again.

"Stop right there and turn around and look at me." There was a new demanding tone to her voice that irritated me even further. I stopped and kicked my foot against the ground. Who was she to be ordering me around anyway?

"I said, turn around. Now!" She sounded really angry. I slowly turned, but couldn't make my eyes meet hers. "Now, I want to know what you said, and I expect an answer."

I snapped my head up and glared straight into her green eyes. "I answered you."

Her eyes flashed and narrowed. "Nothing is not an answer. You said something and I want to know what." I really hadn't said anything I couldn't repeat, but I wasn't going to tell her anything because of the way she demanded it. She couldn't make me talk. "I'm waiting." I pressed my lips tighter together. She'd be waiting for a long time. I heard someone coming down the hall.

"Sarah, I've just had the most wonderful idea." Mrs. Denton

bustled into the room. "I called Harvey Junior, and he is on his way here to show Katie around town. I thought it would be a shame to keep her inside on a day like today."

Hallelujah! Someone was on my side. I watched Sarah's face to see how she would react. I never thought I could be so thankful to a woman who looked like an old gray sheep for butting into my business. Since she had already called Harvey Junior, I didn't see how Sarah could turn down the offer without seeming rude.

Sarah must have thought of that because she seemed to swallow her anger, and forced a smile before answering. "Thank you, Harriet. It was so nice of you to think of Katie, and I think she'll enjoy it. Won't you Katie?" Something in the tone of her voice made me realize she wanted me to thank Mrs. Denton also.

"Yes. Thanks, Mrs. Denton. It's a great idea." What else could I say? I felt uncomfortable because I felt like Sarah wanted more from me. My answer seemed to please Mrs. Denton though because she clasped her hands together and smiled.

"I'm so glad. Junior should be here in a few minutes." With that she bustled back to her office.

Now I had to try to get back on Sarah's good side, and not make her angry before I left. If I did anything to make her angry, she would be able to keep me from going, and I didn't want that to happen. "Thanks, Sarah."

She flung me a sharp look. "I only agreed to make Harriet happy."

She was going to make it difficult. Maybe I should apologize for my earlier attitude, but she had made me so mad. "I know, I'm still glad you said yes." I glanced down at the counter because I couldn't meet her eyes again. "I'm sorry about earlier." She still didn't look too happy. Well, I had done my part. If she wanted to be a grouch, that was her business. At least she had forgotten about grilling me about what I said.

"Katie, I want you to be on your best behavior with Harvey Junior." There she went treating me like a baby again. What did she think I'd do? "Do you understand?" She flipped a lock of her chestnut brown hair back.

"Yes." Why couldn't she trust me? I stared down at the floor.

"Katie, look at me." I gave a sideways glance in her direction. "My reason for asking you to be on your best behavior is not necessarily because I don't trust you, but who you're going with." I leaned on the counter and looked into her clear green eyes. This sounded interesting. "Harvey Junior is not someone I'd normally like you to be going places with."

I'd have to remember that for the future if I needed to come up with a way to upset Sarah. "Why not?"

She looked straight back at me. "He's liable to say some mean things to you, or play some kind of a trick. Regardless of what he says or does, I want you to be nice in return. Remember that you are a McCabe." Remember! No one ever let me forget. "And no smoking or drinking while you're gone either."

"You know about that?" I was sunk. They'd never trust me if they knew about the shed and the flask. I stuffed my hands in my pockets and stomped over to the jewelry box display. Why did Daddy have to say anything? It'd be like being in prison for a year.

I pretended to be interested in a carved wooden box, while looking out the window trying to catch a glimpse of Harvey before he arrived. I spotted a person coming down the street toward the shop. As he drew near, the figure became a short pudgy boy about my age. This must be Harvey. He wore dark blue slacks, somewhat rumpled, a half untucked white shirt, and dirty tennis shoes with untied laces that flopped on the ground as he walked. Just as he turned to come in the door, a lock of frizzy brown hair fell across his eyes, and I noticed beads of sweat across his freckled nose and upper lip. I hoped his personality turned out to be better than his slobbish looks.

Friends and Enemies

"Hey, Sarah. Where's this girl I'm supposed to show around." His voice had that skittery sound of being between a boy's and a man's.

"Katie, come on over." I put down the jewelry box and tried to smile as I walked over. After all, it might be fun. "This is Harvey Denton, Junior. You have a good time looking around, but be back before one." Sarah watched us anxiously as we turned to go out.

Once outside, I spun back around to wave and give Sarah a smile. She stood at the window as if to watch us out of sight.

Though still morning, the heat of the sun could be seen rising in waves from the street. Harvey's face beaded up with sweat as soon as we walked outside. "Where are we going?"

He smoothed back his hair, which had fallen into his eyes again, before answering. "I thought I'd take you to see my old man first. He owns the bank, and just about everything else in town." He sounded smug. I could tell he thought his father owning things made him important. Maybe he was, but to me he sounded like a weasel.

As we stepped off the curb, I marveled at how big and wide the streets were compared to back home.

"Well, Katie McCabe, how do you like it here so far?"

The question startled me. I didn't really care about the town. "I guess it's all right. I haven't given it much thought." I just wanted to go home. "By the way, I go by Katie. You don't have to tack on the last name."

A look passed over his face I couldn't quite define, like he meant to get under my skin and succeeded. "Sure."

At this point, we arrived at the bank. When Harvey opened the door, a blast of cold air came gushing out. Harvey walked coolly past the teller's desk and straight back to the manager's office. Even there he walked right in without knocking, almost as if he owned the bank instead of his father.

"Dad, I brought Katie McCabe to meet you."

Mr. Denton had grizzly, graying hair, and he wore a suit with wide lapels and a string tie. Not exactly the male fashion statement of the century. "How do you do?" He stood to shake my hand, and I saw that he wasn't a very tall man, but thin and wiry. His handshake was strong and aggressive, and I couldn't put him and Mrs. Denton together in my mind.

"Fine, thank you, Mr. Denton."

"Call me H.L. Everybody around here does. Now which of the McCabe boys is your daddy?" He leaned back in his chair as if getting ready for a long chat.

"Sam McCabe."

"Little Sammy?" Little! I always thought of my Daddy as a big man. Certainly bigger than Mr. Denton. "What's he up to now?"

"He's a sheriff."

He picked up a pencil and started tapping it on his hand. "A lawman. That's exactly what you'd expect a McCabe boy to be." I didn't know what to say to that. Harvey didn't help matters any either. I could feel him staring at the back of my head, and it made me uncomfortable. H.L. pursed his lips out underneath his mustache. "A sheriff, that's something to think about. Come to think of it, I do remember something about Sam going into law enforcement. I was kind of surprised he didn't go into the force here." I hoped he wouldn't bring up Mamma. I'm not sure how I would handle hearing about her from a total stranger. "He left these parts suddenly a long time ago and hasn't been back since."

Something didn't make sense. Daddy was on the force here until Mamma died. I couldn't believe Mr. Denton didn't know that, and he must know why Daddy left too.

"Did he come with you? I'd like to see him again. I've known your daddy since he was born." So that explained why he called Daddy, 'little Sammy'. "I expect he told you he grew up in these parts. Your Uncle Charley and I were boys together."

I could imagine Uncle Charley being younger, but not this man. He had the look of being born old, wearing an ugly suit. "I remember Sam always tagging along after Charley trying to be just like him. Oh well, that's enough talk of the past for now." He sat back up to his desk. "I hear Junior is giving you a tour of the town, and I'm sure you want to get on with it." He chuckled. "And I'm sure Junior is anxious to be seen taking a pretty girl like you around town."

I felt sick to my stomach. The things grownups thought and had the nerve to say. "So get along now, and have fun."

I backed toward the door. "Nice to have met you Mr. Denton, I mean H.L. Bye now." I tripped on the doorjamb.

As we walked out of the bank Harvey had a smirk on his face. "Where would you like to go now?"

"You're asking me? I'm the new one here."

Harvey shrugged. "Well, there's not much to see."

Terrific. We would spend the entire time I had left standing on the curb waiting for Harvey to make up his mind on where to go.

"I don't feel like going on a tour of my old man's grocery store, or his barbershop, and his movie house isn't open yet." He paused to wipe the sweat off his forehead. He seemed to be trying to impress me by what his father owned. "I guess we could go over to the park and see who's around. And after that we could go by Dad's malt shop and ask Max to fix us something."

I gave Harvey a hard look. "Is there anything your Dad doesn't own?"

He looked somber for a moment. "He doesn't own your Uncle's construction company." The smug expression returned to his face. "But that's about it."

We were almost to the park, and I could see some guys in the distance playing football. It looked like a nice friendly game, and I wanted to go over closer to watch. I thought Harvey could introduce me to them.   After all, meeting new people was one of the things we were supposed to be doing.

Instead, he stopped beneath the shade of a big tree, leaned up against the trunk, and shoved his hands in his pockets. "In fact, your Uncle is the only one of the McCabe brothers my Dad hasn't been able to run out of town so far. And even so, your cowardly Uncle hides out at that old farm of his most of the time."

I couldn't believe Harvey was talking that way about Uncle Charley. I didn't know him that well yet, but he seemed like a fighter. And from the way Daddy talked about him, he wouldn't run away from things like a coward.

A glint appeared in Harvey's eyes. "Your daddy was the first one he ran out." What on earth was he talking about? Daddy left because he didn't want to be in a place that constantly reminded him of Mamma, so he transferred. "I've heard my Dad say over and over that Sam was the weakest of the McCabe brothers."

"You can stop right there, Harvey Denton Junior. I don't have to listen to things like that." I started walking quickly toward the football players. I couldn't stand to hear anyone say anything against Daddy. I had to get away from him.

"Katie. Wait." I heard him running after me, his feet pounding on the grass. I didn't stop, but slowed my steps. Maybe he wanted to apologize. He caught up and walked beside me, puffing from lack of breath. "Where are you going in such a hurry?"

Anywhere away from him. I stopped and turned to face him. We were almost to where the guys were playing football, so I tried to keep my voice low and under control. I wanted to shout and strike back at him, but I didn't want to make a fool of myself in front of total strangers. "You have no right to be saying things about my Daddy or my Uncle. They're both good men, and you can't say any different." I glared straight into his eyes. "From now on, if you have something bad to say about my family, don't say it around me."

Harvey put his hands on his hips and sneered at me. "Oh yeah? What'll you do if I do say anything?"

I said the first thing that popped into my head. "I just might punch you."

Harvey laughed. "I'd like to see you try. You'd be really sorry for even thinking about taking a swing at me."

I wanted to hit his smug, smiling face, but I remembered what Sarah had said about being nice to Harvey. How could she honestly expect me to be nice to such a creep? But, I think she meant it.

"Just don't push me to it." My anger reached a boiling point, so I concentrated on watching one of the guys catch a pass.

"Such tough words." The jeering tone of his voice made me grit my teeth. "But then again, you're probably weak, just like your daddy. How strong can a guy be that had to run away?" He put his pudgy, sweaty arm around my shoulder and hissed in my ear. "He let the death of your mamma turn him into an emotional cripple." I could feel the warmth of his hot breath going into my ear. "He stopped working and spent every night crying into his beer." He paused and then put his mouth so close to my ear that his lips brushed it. "Sounds pretty weak to me."

I shrugged his arm off, gave him a light shove to get him away from me, and turned to walk away. Then my anger got the better of me. I turned quickly back around and hit him as hard as I could. He walked right into it. He went down flat. I hit him so hard, that I hurt my hand, and had to shake it out to loosen it up. I heard the guys who had been playing football start to cheer. I had a sinking feeling that I made a big mistake.

I reached down to give Harvey a hand up. He slapped my hand away. "Come on Harvey, get up." Harvey pulled himself up to a sitting position, and then sat there rubbing his jaw.

"Hey slugger! Why don't you do that again?"

If I had to do something stupid, why did I have to do it in front of an audience? I tried to act like it didn't bother me. "The show's over for today."

Harvey crawled over by a tree, probably to get away from me, and stood up. One of the guys had walked over and stood quietly beside me. He motioned for his friends to stop. "I'd like to shake the hand of the person who finally put Harvey Denton in his place."

How embarrassing. I didn't want to be known as a tomboy, or a slugger, or anything like that. "I didn't mean to. He just made me mad, and I lost my temper." To make things worse, this guy was cute; tall with dark brown hair and eyes, and a nice sensitive-looking face. His body was muscular, probably from playing football.

"I know. You've done what we've all been itching to do for a long time." He smiled a nice, almost shy smile. "My name's Tom Pike, what's yours?"

"Katie." Harvey stamped back and forth nearby, glaring at me when he could catch my eye.

"Katie what?"

Here we went again. I'd say my last name and he'd expect me to fit into the McCabe mold. "Katie McCabe."

His smile got bigger, and he seemed amused. "Well, Katie, I'll just have to watch out for that McCabe right hook of yours, because I think we'll be seeing a lot of each other, that is if you're going to be sticking around town for awhile."

"Really?" A warm feeling started to well up inside me. Maybe I hadn't blown things as bad as I thought. "I'm starting school here next week." Tom moved a little closer.

"Really. In fact, I'd like to take you around and show you the town, show you the school and a few other places, and then we'll finish up by going to Max's for a shake."

Harvey shoved his way in between us. "I'm taking her, Tom."

Tom's face darkened with a scowl. "Look, she doesn't have to stay with you, and I don't think she wants to."

Harvey's eyes narrowed. "Well, I guess I'll just have to go back to the shop then, and explain to Sarah where Katie is." His face got a mean look to it.

I had a sudden vision of Sarah tracking me down at Max's and dragging me out in front of everyone to take me back to the store. I couldn't live through something like that. I wouldn't be able to look anyone in the eye because I knew what they'd be thinking. I couldn't let Harvey do that to me. His back was already turned, and he started walking off in the direction of the street.

It would cost me a great deal of pride to call him back, but I was starting to panic. I just hoped Tom would understand. "Harvey, don't go yet."

When he turned around, his grin was twisted and distorted from the swelling of his jaw. I got a sick feeling in the pit of my stomach. I didn't know I'd hurt him so much. My hand started to throb again as I stared at his face. I looked down at my hand and saw that it was swelling too. Just what I needed. Harvey's face beat up and the evidence that I had done it marked my hand. "Let's get some ice for your face. It looks terrible."

Harvey's mean little grin faded and he shook his head. "I don't want anything for it." Because of the swelling, he had to speak slowly, and even then his words were slurred. I barely understood what he said.

"Tom, shouldn't we do something?" I needed someone to back me up. I felt like I ought to do something about his jaw, even if I wasn't sorry I hit him.

Tom shook his head. "We can't make him do something he doesn't want to do." I guess I couldn't. I also had to figure a way to keep Harvey from rushing back to the store, and to keep Tom from leaving at the same time. Tom put his hand on my shoulder. "Why don't you just let him go?"

"I can't. It'd make things worse." Shaking my head, I kept my voice low because I didn't want Harvey to hear that he had a hold on me in any way. "My cousin Sarah wouldn't understand."

"I know Sarah. She seems a pretty understanding sort." I shook my head and bit my lip. Not with me she wasn't. Tom cleared his throat. "All right. What do you want to do then? We can't stand here doing nothing for the rest of the day."

Exactly what I had been trying to figure out. "Let me see if I can talk to Harvey. We'll go down by the lake and you and your friends can practice somewhere close by."

A smile lit up his face. "That sounds good. Just don't talk to Harvey for too long."

"Don't worry." Who was he kidding? The sooner I could get away from the little creep, the better. Tom ran off in the direction of his friends and yelled to one of them to throw him a pass.

Harvey seemed to gloat when he saw Tom running off. "I thought that guy would never leave. You don't want to spend too much time with him."

I had to remember to keep control over my temper this time. I couldn't let him get the best of me. Slowly, I took a deep breath. "Can't we try to get along?"

"With that guy?" Harvey gave a derisive laugh. "You've got to be crazy. I don't hang around with people like him."

Tom would probably say the same thing about Harvey, with more reason. I picked up a stone and skipped it across the water. "Look, Harvey, I wanted you to know I'm really sorry about hitting you." I almost gagged on the apology. Harvey shrugged and rubbed his jaw some more. I shuddered to think what would happen when Sarah found out, but I wanted to stay away from the store for as long as possible. "Do you want to go to the malt shop now? An ice cold drink would do you some good."

"Let's just wait a little bit."

Why did he want to wait? He wasn't going to take me anywhere else, and with his jaw so swollen he wasn't saying very much. He started picking up stones and trying to skip them across the lake. He turned his back and made it plain that he didn't want to talk to me. I went over to a big tree and sat down underneath it. Tom glanced over at me and I shrugged.

I felt like I could sit back and relax for the rest of the day. With the sun filtering through the leaves of the tree, the rays danced gently on my face. I closed my eyes and felt the tension drain from me. I'd been really keyed up. I felt a shadow cross me and opened my eyes to see Harvey standing over me.

"Do you want to go out in a boat?"

I paused before answering, and then shook my head. "I'd have to check with Sarah first." I wouldn't mind going out on the lake, but I didn't want to go with Harvey. If he had his way, I'd end up at the bottom of the lake.

"Let's go then." He started walking off without waiting for me to get up. I looked around for Tom and tried to catch his eye, but he and his friends were not there anymore. As we walked down the street, Harvey stayed a few steps ahead of me and as far over to the side as he could get, as if he didn't want to be near me at all. I could understand some of it. His jaw hurt a lot, but he deserved it for the things he said about my family.

As we passed the bank, Harvey started to walk even faster. When we got to Max's, he went straight in and up to the counter to talk to the man behind it. I couldn't hear what was said because I was too far away, and Harvey spoke in a low tone. A voice came from behind me. "Hey slugger."

I spun around. "Tom!" Happy to see him again, I smiled. "Where did you go? I looked around for you and your friends, but you disappeared."

"It didn't look like you were having any luck with Harvey, so I thought it would be better if he thought we left. I figured we would catch up to you here." He stopped speaking and glared over my shoulder. Harvey was standing right behind me.

"What do you want to eat or drink?"

"Nothing, thanks. I don't have any money with me." I felt somewhat self-conscious by having to say that, but I didn't want him to ask why. That would have been worse.

"I already fixed it with Max, so go ahead and order what you want."

"Thanks, Harvey." Maybe he did have a good side to him. I was a little surprised by it though. We walked over to the counter and sat down. Tom's friends came in a couple of minutes later and joined us.

"Katie, I'd like you to meet my friends Mike and Pete."

Mike reminded me of a big huggable teddy bear with blonde shaggy hair, and a crooked smile. Pete was the shortest of the three, and even he stood taller than Harvey. He wore glasses that magnified his eyes, and his short dark hair was combed neatly to the side.

Mike ran a hand through his hair. "So, are you here for a visit, or are you moving here?"

Just the question I wanted to avoid. I couldn't answer that I didn't want to stay, but I had to answer somehow. "I guess you could say that I'm moving here. I'll be living with my Uncle Charley during the school year."

"Great. We'll all be going to the high school together then."

Max brought my chocolate malt over, and I sipped on it while Mike continued. "Tom and I will be juniors this year, and Pete will be a sophomore." I knew they had to be older than I was. "What class will you be?"

"I'll be a lowly freshman." Well, at least I had connections in the upper class. "What class will you be in, Harvey?"

Harvey turned his head and refused to answer. Tom grinned. "Ol' Harv'll be a freshman too."

Terrific. We might even get stuck in some of the same classes together. "Do you have good teachers?"

All three of the guys shrugged. Mike stopped drinking his Coke. "Some are better than others. The same as any other school I guess."

Max brought over their burgers and fries. Tom picked up his meal and cocked his head to one side. "Let's move to a booth."

"Okay." I stood up and started toward a booth. Harvey sat and played with a fry, ignoring the rest of us. "Are you coming, Harvey?"

He shook his head. What more could I do? I tried to talk to him. I asked him to join us. But he wouldn't cooperate at all.

"I'm a little worried about starting school here. This will be the first time I've ever gone to a new school, and I'm sure yours is a lot bigger than mine. Plus, I don't know anyone."

Tom sat down next to me. "Hey, you know us. We'll take care of you."

Mike started laughing. "Anyone who has a right jab like her doesn't need to be taken care of. She can do it herself." He stopped laughing and a very serious expression crossed his face. "Maybe I should get you to be my bodyguard."

I knew I had blown it with that punch. I felt myself starting to blush.

"Come on Mike, give the girl a break." Tom reached across the table and lightly slapped the back of Mike's head. Lowering his voice, he leaned forward. "All of us have wanted to do the same to Harvey at one time or another. She just beat us to it."

Pete offered me some of his fries. "We'll be glad to be your protectors, Katie." He smiled shyly at me, and looked a little self-conscious for having said anything.

"I'll just call you my Musketeers." I finished my malt and looked at my watch. I only had ten minutes to get back to the shop. I looked around for Harvey, but he wasn't around anymore. "I have to get back now. See you later."

"I'll walk you back, Katie." Tom got up with me and started walking over to the door.

When we got to the door, a plate banged on the counter. "Hey! Where do you think you're going?" My head whipped around. Max was leaning forward, his fists bunched on the countertop. He didn't look very happy either. "You can't leave until you pay for the hamburger, fries, and malt."

"Pay for it?" Tom had already paid for his, so this must be Harvey's petty little way of getting back at me for having hit him. "Harvey told me he would take care of it for me." I didn't even have a hamburger and fries. He must have stuck me for both his and my bill.

Max frowned. "He told me when you walked through the door that you would be paying the bill." That little snake.

Tom reached for his wallet. "How much is it, Max?"

"Five bucks."

I couldn't get over how sweet Tom was being. I was determined to get even with Harvey for this stunt. "Thanks, Tom. I'll pay you back as soon as I can." I had no idea when that would be, because I had no way of earning any money.

He held the door open for me. "Don't think of it. It's my treat."

I gave a little laugh. "Looks like you get to be a Musketeer for me already. Still, you shouldn't have to pay for Harvey too."

Tom waved his hand in the air. "Don't worry about it."

"Well, if you won't let me pay you back, I'll have to let you know how I extract my revenge on Harvey."

Tom stopped. "We're having football practice tomorrow morning at the school; will you come and watch, and cheer us on?"

I really wanted to be able to, but I didn't know if I would even be in town the next morning. "If I can, I'll be there."

"Great." A smile lit up Tom's face.

I had a feeling Sarah would be keeping tabs on me and where I was going, so I wanted to get her to like Tom. That way I'd be able to see him as often as I could. "Would you like to walk me back to the shop?" I smiled up at him. "Then you could explain that Harvey left me, so you kindly walked me back." That ought to make a good impression on Sarah.

It seemed to be the perfect plan, except just before we got to the shop, out walked Harvey. "Come on Katie, you'll be late if we don't hurry up."

"Forget it, Harvey."

He shrugged his shoulders and turned away. "It's your funeral."

I kept forgetting that he could say anything once he walked through the door. I couldn't let him have a head start because then he'd get to tell his side of the fight first. "Harvey! Wait." I had to yell for him to hear me.

"Let him go." Tom put his hand on my shoulder.

"I can't, Tom." This was so hard for me. I wanted to stay with Tom, but I knew that I couldn't. "I can't allow Harvey to get the jump on me. Especially since I hit him, I can't trust anything that he might say."

Disappointment covered Tom's face. "I'm sorry. I forgot about the fight." He shook his head. "Besides you couldn't trust Harvey further than you could throw him while he was carrying a two hundred pound bag of wet cement, even before you knocked him flat."

"Are you coming or what?" Harvey had not budged one inch from where he stopped.

"I gotta go. Thanks for everything Tom and I'll see you around."

"You can count on that."

Leaving Tom, I jogged down the street until I caught up with Harvey. "That was a mean, rotten, low down, jerk of a trick you played on me back at the malt shop." I paused to catch my breath. "What do you have to say for yourself?"

He gave me a fake innocent look. "Me? You were the one talking to those other guys, and I figured if they wanted your company, they could pay for it too."

My anger started to rise again. "What a liar you are. You told Max that I would be picking up the tab for both of us, after you made sure I didn't have any money." I swallowed hard so I wouldn't lose my temper again. "That's not only cheap, it's disgusting."

He smirked and shrugged. "So? What are you going to do about it?" I knew what I'd like to do.

"We'd better go in or you'll be late." I'd already be in trouble for hitting Harvey, what difference would it make if I got in a little more for walking in the door late?

Sarah had her back to us as we entered the shop. "It's about time you two. I'll be with you in a minute." When she turned around, the smile of greeting quickly faded from her face and her hand flew up to her mouth. "My goodness Harvey, what on earth happened to your face?"

Now I'd get it. Harvey pulled himself up as tall as he could make himself, kind of a losing battle I thought, and looked like he was going to try and bluster his way through the story of what happened. "Some guys down by the lake started picking on Katie, and I tried to stop them." What? I couldn't believe my ears. "There were three of them and they started by making rude remarks and then things got worse. One of them started stroking her hair, even though she told them to stop and tried to walk away. Then another of the guys caught her and forced her to hug him. She was struggling to get away, so I grabbed one of their arms and then they all got mad. One of them held me with my arms behind my back while the other two started to hit me."

I just stared at Harvey. I think I was going into shock. "Katie started screaming, so they let go of me and ran off." I still couldn't believe it. I expected him to say right out that I hit him, and then sit back and watch me squirm.

"That's awful." Sarah took a closer look at his jaw. "Go on back to the office and let your mother take care of it. If she needs me to, I'll stay until she's had a chance to ice it to get the swelling down."

"No, you go ahead. I'll be all right."

Sarah still looked pretty horrified with the damage that was done. She turned to me. "Katie, are you okay?" Sarah seemed to believe the story, unbelievable as it was. Maybe I was off the hook after all. "Did you get the names of the boys who did this?"

I started to shake my head when Harvey decided to stick the knife in and twist it. "I think it was Tom Pike and his buddies. I'm not sure because I don't really know them that well, but I think it was them." My jaw dropped. What a filthy, rotten, lying, scumbag. No word I could think of was too bad for Harvey.

Sarah looked very concerned. "I know Tom, and that just doesn't sound like something he'd do. He's always seemed like a very nice, polite boy."

Harvey tried to give her a world-wise expression, but the swelling caused his face to twist into a grimace. "You'd be surprised how much he has changed now that he's on the varsity football squad. He thinks he can do anything he wants, just because he might be the starting quarterback this year."

Sarah put her arm across my shoulders and gave me a quick squeeze. "I'm so sorry that something like this had to happen on your first day in town. Uncle Charley will be very upset, and I wouldn't be surprised if he didn't go and visit Tom's parents."

This was getting worse and worse. "No. I'm fine. Really." I barely stammered the words out.

"Well, we'll talk about it later. I can't thank you enough Harvey for looking after Katie for us."

I was at a complete and total loss of how to start fixing this whole mess. If I had called Harvey out on his lie right at the beginning, it would have been better, but I was speechless. I didn't even know what to say. And then the little creep decided to throw Tom and his friends, who had been perfect gentlemen, unlike the slimy Harvey, into the mix and it felt like the whole thing was spiraling out of control. For once in my life, I wasn't getting into trouble for something I had done wrong, but this was even worse. Daddy would have asked me right away if I had done it. But then again, he knew I had a habit of getting into fights.

Confessions

A fter doing some errands in town, and a little grocery shopping, Sarah and I returned to the farm. I helped her put the groceries away and then had a bit of free time, the first I'd had since arriving. I hadn't been able to think of a solution yet to undo the mess that Harvey created that didn't involve a full confession on my part. Sarah had pulled out a text book for a class that she was taking so she could do some studying. As she put the book down on the table, I tried to pull my courage together.

"Sarah? Is it okay if I call my Daddy?" I knew that if I could just talk to Daddy, he would help me fix this mess. He'd be upset with me, but he would at least listen and know that my story was the truth and help me get things set straight. I didn't want Tom to get into trouble based on such a despicable lie. I wouldn't be able to live with myself if that happened.

Her eyes were sad as she looked up at me. "I wish you could call your Daddy, honey, but he's in the hospital having tests done and won't be able to talk to you until later. He promised to call as soon as he could." She must have seen the disappointment on my face. "If he hasn't called by then, we'll try giving him a call after supper. His tests should be over for the day by then."

"Okay." I looked down at the floor. I was going to have to try and figure out how to explain this whole situation myself. Maybe I could just talk to Uncle Charley about it. "Do you mind if I go for a walk around the farm?"

She shook her head. "Just be back in time for supper."

Uncle Charley seemed to have a lot of land attached to the farm. They had quite a few animals, a pasture for grazing, and a nice garden where they grew a lot of their own food. I walked past the pasture into the woods surrounding the property, and it gave me a sense of peace. Here I could be myself with no one to pester or bother me. A little clearing by the stream that ran through the property reminded me of my special place at home. It was the place where Timmy and I went when we had things to discuss or trouble to run from. It was a good place for thinking.

I sat down and leaned up against the trunk of a tree. I kept trying to figure out why Harvey told such a twisted and evil lie. I don't know what I would have done if he had just said that I hit him straight out. Maybe tried to explain and make excuses. But when he lied like that, I didn't know what to say. He made himself sound like some kind of mini hero, and he was nothing like one in reality.

I really liked Tom; he was so sweet and nice. After all, it wasn't every guy who would pick up the tab on the spur of the moment like that. It was especially nice when it wasn't just for me, but for the worm-like Harvey too. It made me sick to think that Tom might actually be accused of doing the things Harvey said he did. I had to figure out some way to get Harvey back for that stunt. I needed some method of revenge, where I could include Tom, and preferably something painful. I'd think of something. I always did. Maybe even Mike and Pete could get into the act. I'm sure Harvey had done something in the past to wrong them as well.

In the distance, I heard my name being called. I gave a start and sat upright. I didn't know how long I had been in the clearing, but the darkness of the sky told me that it had been longer than I thought. I brushed the dirt and tree leaves off my pants and hurried back to the house. As I was going, I heard my name called out again.

"Coming."

Sarah stood by the kitchen garden with her hands on her hips waiting for me to get a little closer. "I wasn't sure where you had disappeared to."

I shrugged. "I was just looking around."

She put her arm across my shoulder. "That's fine. I need your help in the kitchen now, so go in and get washed up."

"Work, work, work. That's all you want me to do."

She laughed and gave me a slight swat. "Just get washed up."

As we were getting supper ready, Sarah kept talking about Harvey. "I just can't get over the way he stood up for you today. I think he's beginning to grow up." She pressed her lips together and gave her head a little shake. "I'm still so surprised about Tom though. I never in a million years would think that he would do something like that."

My stomach gave a little lurch. Over and over again, I kept hearing how wonderful Harvey was and how disturbing the news was about Tom. I was starting to get a little panicky about how I was going to straighten this whole thing out without getting myself into trouble. If possible, I wanted everyone to understand why I reacted the way I did. It would have been easier if I had disputed his story right away, but I felt like I got the wind knocked out of me and couldn't catch my breath. Harvey, the most disgusting person I had met in my life, was being glorified into some kind of a hero for something he never did. I wondered what Sarah would be saying if she knew the full truth of the matter. That he had insulted the family, and I hit him because of it. My knuckles were still swollen from the impact. Then when he added the further snake-like act of lying about the whole incident and implicating innocent people, I felt like I could have killed him, but had to listen to how great and changed he was instead.

After supper had been cleared, we all settled into chairs to talk about how the day had gone. Apparently it was some kind of family tradition. I wanted to call Daddy, but was told I could call him a little later so that I could have some privacy for my call.

Of course, Uncle Charley, being the head of the family began. "We got behind schedule again because the concrete didn't set right."

Mark jumped up and started pacing. "I still think it's the stuff we bought from H.L.'s hardware store. It just doesn't mix the right way." Anger smoldered in his eyes. "I think he must monkey around with it before he sells it. Kind of like watering it down, so he can sell more for less cost to him."

Uncle Charley frowned. "Now Mark, I've told you before about making accusations that you can't prove. I agree the concrete we bought this last time is not what it should be, but we don't know where it got tampered with or who did it."

"Well, you know he's doing it. That's just the kind of crook he is." Like son, like father?

Matt looked like he was going to say something, but Uncle Charley continued before he got the chance. "When you can prove that, then we can talk."

Mark scowled and flopped down in his chair. Matt, trying to smooth things over, turned toward Sarah. "How did things go for you and Katie today?"

"Well things were kind of quiet at the shop today, but Katie had some excitement. Why don't you tell them about it?"

I looked down at the floor. Just the thing I didn't know how to get into. The last thing I wanted to talk about was the heroism of Harvey, and if I let Sarah get started, that's what she would go on about. "It was really nothing."

"Nothing! Katie, you can't pretend it didn't happen. The best way to deal with it is meet it head on." She settled back in her chair. "Harvey Junior took Katie on a tour of the town while I was working today. Harriet called him and asked him to, so Katie wouldn't have to sit in the shop all day."

Mark sat up a little straighter. "You actually let her go with that little weasel?"

"I was a little wary at first, but then decided not much could happen in a few hours. Besides, I didn't want to disappoint Harriet. And Harvey showed himself to be a different boy than I thought."

"What do you mean?" Mark sharply rapped out the question.

"Well, believe it or not, some of the boys in town started to pick on Katie, and from Harvey's description they were getting close to assault, and Harvey came to the rescue. He even took a blow to the jaw that made it swell up terribly. He's going to be sore for quite a few days from it."

Everyone started talking at once.

Matt looked skeptical. "I didn't think Harvey would have it in him to do that. The story sounds a little fishy to me."

Mark folded his arms across his chest and stood up. "Who are these boys? I'll need to go have a word with them."

Uncle Charley very quietly took part in the conversation, almost like he was talking to himself. "It just goes to show that good can be found in everyone."

It was too much for me. "Not in him there isn't." The words slipped out a little louder than I intended and everyone stopped talking to stare at me.

Sarah looked a little startled. "What do you mean there isn't any good in him? He fought for you today!"

I took a deep breath. It was now or never. "Things didn't happen exactly the way Harvey said they did."

Matt looked triumphant. "I knew it couldn't be as good as Sarah was painting it."

Sarah continued to press me. "Do you mean he stretched the facts a bit? It's understandable under the circumstances perhaps to do a little exaggerating."

Stretched the facts! He never even touched one of them. "Not exactly." I rubbed my forehead. "No one was picking on me."

"Harvey just got into a fight?" Disbelief was written all over her face.

"In a way." He was definitely the one who started it.

Uncle Charley caught my eyes and held them. "Katie, I think we'd better have the whole story."

I had to figure out where to begin to clean up this mess. "Harvey did get in a fight." That was the only part of the story he told that was true. "Things didn't happen they way he said, though. He started the fight, and I finished it." There was total silence in the room while they all just stared at me like they couldn't believe their ears. "While we were headed down to the lake, Harvey started putting down Daddy, Uncle Charley, and the whole family. I tried to ignore it, but when he started saying things about my Mamma, it just got to be too much." I paused to take a deep breath. There was no turning back now. "So, I hit him." Shock etched itself on each face.

"You?" Sarah faltered. "You did that damage to Harvey's face?" She shook her head. "I don't believe it."

Terrific, tell the truth and no one believes you. "Why would I lie?" What was I doing even trying to explain? "Do you want me to get some witnesses?"

She closed her eyes for a moment and looked like she was in pain. "His face looked so bad; it looked like more than one person did the damage. How many times did you hit him?"

"Just the once. I hit him pretty hard, though." I made it count.

She gazed intensely into my face. "So, the story of those boys attacking you. . . " Her voice trailed off.

"Never happened." I rapped the words out like I was trying to hammer them home.

Concern covered her like a veil, and I could tell that she was still struggling with belief. "I'm having a hard time with understanding why Harvey would have invented an attack on you that didn't happen." She paused. "If you were attacked in that way, you might have felt helpless, and by telling us that it never happened and in fact were the aggressor in the situation might give you a sense of control that you so desperately need right now."

I jumped up and thrust my fist out in front of her. "Look at my hand. How did my knuckles get so swollen?" Marching over to the mantle, I gripped the edge and tried to regain some control. "Harvey is a twisted little creep and I can only guess at why he would have told such a warped story." Inspiration struck me. "He's the one who felt helpless and wanted to make it seem like he wasn't. Who wants to get knocked flat by a girl in front of three of the high school football team players?" Another thought flashed through my mind. "That's why he invented the attack on me. He saw me making friends with people he's never been able to be friends with, so he put me in a position where I would have to let him blame my new friends, or rat myself out." I turned around to face the family again. "I can't stand by and let someone be falsely accused, even if I have to tattle on myself."

Uncle Charley sat there tensing his jaw, so I knew he was not pleased. "Katie, on the one hand, I don't like that you were involved in a fight." He held up his hand as I opened my mouth. "Violence is not something that I condone, and I don't want it happening again." He leaned forward in his chair. "On the other hand, I'm proud of you for standing up for your friends and telling the truth." He looked over at Sarah. "You need to tell Katie what her punishment is for hitting Harvey."

"Me?" Sarah sounded incredulous.

"Katie was under your care when this incident occurred and she needs to know that you have the authority to discipline unacceptable behavior." Sarah continued to look at Uncle Charley in disbelief. "If you don't, anything you say to her in the future won't carry any weight. Your words will simply be an empty threat."

Sarah still didn't look very sure about the whole thing, but she turned toward me. Now I would get it. She thought for a moment. "Since you had enough excess energy to hit Harvey so hard, we'll have to work on getting rid of some of it. Tomorrow, instead of going into town with me, you will stay here and clean out the pig sty." How gross. "Scrub the trough and re-slop it." Disgusting. "Give Günter a bath." How much more could she give me to do? "Muck out the floor of the chicken coop, and put fresh straw down." More. "And scrub the bathroom from floor to ceiling to my satisfaction."

That sure wouldn't be easy. At least she seemed to have come to the end of her list. "Is that all?"

She clenched her jaw. "Yes."

Matthew frowned in thought. "Doesn't Katie have to take the entrance exam for school in the morning?"

"That's right, I forgot." Sarah didn't look very pleased about it. "That's before I have to go to work, so we'll go in, Katie can take her test and I'll have a chance to bring her back here before going in. I scheduled it early so there would be time to spare."

Great, just what I wanted to do. Take a test and then come back and work like a slave all day long. Not all day, because Sarah would probably be back some time tomorrow in the afternoon, and knowing her, she'd expect me to be finished by the time she got back, or close to it.

Uncle Charley stood up. "I'm going to give Sam a call now, so we'll give Katie some privacy."

My heart leapt into my throat. I missed my Daddy so much; it was almost more than I could stand. As Mark passed by, he ruffled my hair and gave me an amused look. "I knew you were a hellion, Kit-Kat." He leaned over and whispered in my ear. "I know something about Junior, and I'm sure he deserved what you dished out, so don't worry too much about it."

Uncle Charley held out the phone. "I have your Daddy on the line."

I took the receiver from Uncle Charley and he left the room. "Hi, Daddy."

"Hi Katie, how are you doing?" His voice sounded scratchy and was very weak. He cleared his throat. "These tests they are doing are giving me cotton mouth." He sounded a little stronger, but not much.

"I'm doing fine." It hit me all of a sudden that he was very sick. I couldn't start telling him how much I wanted to come home. I had to focus on positive things, so he wouldn't have to worry about me. "I've already made some friends." I didn't need to bring up that I had made an enemy as well. "And tomorrow I have to take the entrance exam for high school." What else could I tell him? My mind was racing for positive things to share. "I let Sarah cut my bangs, so they're not in my face anymore." Not willingly, but he didn't need to know that either.

"Tell Sarah, my hat's off to her. She got you to do something I never could." His laugh turned into a wracking cough. I could hear him taking a sip of water. "I'm glad you called because I need to talk to you."

All of a sudden I didn't want to hear what he had to say. I knew in my heart it wasn't good news. "Why don't we wait until your tests are finished and you're feeling better?"

There was a moment of silence from the other end of the phone. "Sometimes we have to face things that we don't want to, and this is one of those times." I could feel tears starting to prick my eyes. "I wanted to be able to tell you this in person, and not over the phone, but right now I think it's best to tell you what the doctors have to say.

The results from my tests so far are not very good. They still have a few more to do, but they are being done to find out the extent of the illness." Hot tears started running down my face. I couldn't stop them. "There's no easy way to tell you this, Katie." His voice cracked. "I have an inoperable cancer."

He waited a moment, but I couldn't say anything because I felt like my tears were choking me. "I'm going to fight this as hard as I can, so I need you to be strong for me. As soon as they release me from here, I'll come out and spend some time with you at the farm." He took another sip of water. "So, I'll see you in a few days. I love you very much, Katie."

"I love you too Daddy and I miss you so much." The words came out in a whisper, which was all I could manage at the moment. After I hung up the phone, I sat there feeling numb. I couldn't get my mind to focus on what I had just been told.

Uncle Charley came into the room and sat down quietly next to me. He didn't say anything, just patted my hand and let me cry. I'm glad he didn't try and tell me everything was going to be okay. I felt like nothing was ever going to be okay again. I couldn't stop the silent stream of tears that continued to fall. "He told you?" My voice croaked like a frog.

Uncle Charley nodded. "I told Matt, Mark, and Sarah as well." His strong arms encircled me in a tight hug. "I don't know what to say, other than I am here if you need me."

I buried my wet face into the front of his shirt and he held me and patted my back until I stopped crying. My Daddy wanted me to be strong for him, so I'd better pull myself together and at least try. "Tomorrow promises to be a long day, so I'd better get some sleep." I stood up and turned to leave the room.

"Katie." I stopped and looked back. Uncle Charley swallowed hard, like he was biting back words. "I know it might be hard, but try and get some rest." Somehow, I didn't believe that those were the words he was going to say when he called me back.

As I entered our room, Sarah looked up from the text book she was studying, and I could tell that she had been crying too. Emotionally I was wrung out and I really didn't want to talk, about anything. She seemed to understand without my having to say a word. I grabbed one of my books. After a day like this one, I needed to escape into a fantasy world, where all of the problems were not mine. I could escape and not have to think.

Morning came a little bit easier this time, and I found myself falling into the routine of things. I didn't know whether I liked that or not. Sarah and I had to leave around seven so I could take the entrance exam for high school. I was glad to have a reason not to have to think about anything else.

I didn't think much of Mr. Conway, the principal. He dressed like an old grandpa, but wasn't old enough to be one, even though he was balding at the top of his head. He seemed to fuss a lot about nothing. Whether the pencil that he had given me was the correct type for the test, if I understood the directions and time limits, and what I was supposed to do when I was through. I just wished he would leave so I could take my test in peace and get it over with.

I finished early, and Sarah went in to talk to Mr. Conway about my past school record and what classes would be best for me. So, I wandered out on the campus to have a look around. I saw the football field in the distance and wondered if Tom was out there practicing. I could see a bunch of players and the coach was yelling something at them, so I went over to take a closer look.

After a pass play, Tom looked over to the sidelines where I stood, and waved. I grinned and waved madly back. At least I had been able to make it for part of the practice. Just when it looked like they might be taking a short break, I heard Sarah calling me. With one last longing look toward Tom, I broke into a run to the truck. Time to go home and enter into slavery.

After reminding me of my jobs, Sarah left. It shouldn't be too bad, and if I worked quickly enough I might be able to get some time to myself to read or something. I still didn't want any time to think because I couldn't cope. The first thing I had to do was figure out which awful job to do first. The bathroom probably, because after working around pigs I would definitely need to shower off, and I wanted to shower after getting completely through with everything. After that, I'd probably give Günter his bath, clean up the chicken coop, and then deal with the pigs.

Cleaning the bathroom went well. I got hot while working, but I didn't have any problems with it. I went out to the barn and got out the big metal tub Sarah had shown me. I took it down from its peg and filled it up. I grabbed the shampoo from the shelf and set it beside the tub. Now all I had to do was find Günter. I didn't know anything about him, so I didn't have the slightest clue where to start looking. The only thing I could do was call him and hope that he came.

"Günter." I heard him barking in the distance, but it didn't sound like he was coming closer. I tried yelling a little louder. "Günter. Come on boy."

This time I heard him crashing through the woods, and soon I could hear his paws hitting the ground. When he got close to me, I grabbed onto his collar and walked toward the tub. He sat down and dug his feet into the ground. "Come on. Get up."

I felt like I was dragging a hundred pound sack of flour, but that would have been easier. I finally got him into the tub, but he wouldn't stay. When Sarah told me to give Günter a bath, she didn't tell me I would be in a wrestling match. He was so big that he could do just about anything he wanted to, and I couldn't stop him.

"Günter sit." I forced his back end down in the water. I quickly grabbed the shampoo and lathered him up. Just when I was getting ready to rinse him off, he stood up, shook himself and jumped out of the tub. Once out he stopped long enough to shake himself off again, and he got soap in my eye.

It burned like crazy. For a minute I couldn't open my eyes, which were both watering so much I felt like I was crying. As soon as I could force them open enough, I went over to the hose and washed out my eyes. The water felt good on my face, but my vision was still blurry even after I washed the soap out. I still had to find Günter again and rinse him off.

He came quickly this time, and I hosed him off instead of trying to get him back into the tub. I towel dried him and combed out the tangles as quickly as I could. It had taken longer to give him his bath than I thought it would, and I wanted to get done with all my extra jobs as soon as I possibly could. I could still get done early if I worked fast.

It shouldn't take too long to clean out the chicken coop.

I figured the best way to do it was to rake out the floor, then put down the fresh straw. As I raked, I decided to focus on what I was going to do to Harvey. It was much easier to face thinking about revenge, than what was happening with my Daddy. I couldn't hit him again. Besides, slow torture of some kind would be the best. Either that or find some way to embarrass him in front of his friends, like he did to me.

I thought my heart was going to stop when Max asked me to pay for the food. If Tom hadn't paid for it, I don't know what I would have done. Since I was new to the town, Max wouldn't have accepted my word that I would pay him as soon as I could. I didn't even know where I would have gotten the money from. I'd have had to ask Sarah for some, and I don't think she'd have liked that, and I know I wouldn't.

Not concentrating on what I was doing, I didn't see the egg on the ground until after I hit it with the rake. The shell cracked and an awful smell filled the coop. My eyes started watering again and my stomach began to heave. I rushed outside to get a breath of fresh air. Great. One more thing to slow me down. It had been my own carelessness, but it still made me mad.

The morning was half over, and I still had the worst job to go. I wondered what would happen if I just decided not to do any more. What would they do to me? Oh well, the day had to end sometime. I snatched the rake up again and went back inside. The smell wasn't quite as bad, so I finished as quickly as I could with the raking. As I put the straw down, my thoughts went back to Harvey. I didn't know enough about him to get him back good. There had to be some way.

Sarah told me that the town picnic was tomorrow. That would be a good place to embarrass Harvey, if I could. It would not only be in front of his friends, if he had any, but in front of the whole town. I wanted to be careful though. I didn't want to get in trouble this time, and Harvey really deserved it.

I finished with the chicken coop and moved on to the pig sty. Uncle Charley only kept three pigs. It was amazing how much mess so few pigs could make. Around the trough, the ground was muddy and slimy from the food that had spilled from it. The pigs squealed as I stepped into the sty. One of them ran over and tried to rub up against me. Somehow, I didn't think this was how every girl wanted to spend one of the last days of summer vacation. I knew it wasn't my idea of a fun time. Still, it had to be done.

I decided to scrub out the trough first. That way, I wouldn't have to back track and clean up anything I dropped from it. As I got closer, the smell began to nauseate me. Sour milk seemed to be one of the pigs' favorite dishes. After getting so close to food like this, I doubted whether I would want to eat dinner, let alone touch any lunch.

It went all right until one of the pigs decided it was hungry. It pushed up against me to get some food, and some of the slop spilled on me. I smelled so bad I couldn't stand to be near myself. I hoped that plenty of hot water and soap would take the smell away.

I didn't realize the amount of time that had gone by while working on the pig sty. There was just no fast way to clean out a pig sty. Most of the time was spent on scrubbing the trough trying to get it clean. It didn't look like it had been done for five years at least. I scrubbed until my hand and arm ached. I tried to use the other hand, but somehow it didn't seem to work as well.

I heard Sarah's truck pull up in the drive. I wanted to be finished by the time she got back, so I wouldn't have to have her standing over me telling me how to do the job right. I stood up to tell her that I was almost finished, but I didn't see the pig underneath my feet. I stepped forward and accidentally put my foot down on the pig. It jumped and squealed so loud, it sounded like I was killing it. Surprised, I lost my balance and fell front first into the slimy mud. Mud splattered on my face when I hit the ground. The rest of me was covered with mud. I was so busy picking myself up out of the mud and staring at the mess, that I didn't see Sarah come up.

"If you do that again, I'll go get the camera and take your picture. Maybe I should take it right now anyway."

I sat up on my knees. I had a choice. I could either get mad because she thought it was funny, or I could laugh with her. "If you do, I'll pull you in here with me. We could have a mud fight." I decided getting mad wouldn't change anything.

Sarah laughed out loud now. "I'm sorry. I can't help it. You look like Brer Rabbit's tar baby with all that mud on you."

I stood up and walked over to the fence. "I must look pretty funny." With my hand I put some mud on her nose. "I thought you might look good in a mud pack. It's always in fashion, and it's supposed to be excellent for the skin."

She backed quickly away. "Before we both end up with mud all over us, I'd better go in the house. I'll put some clean clothes in the bathroom for you, so you don't have to track mud all through the house."

After she left, it didn't take long for me to finish up. I went around to the back of the house, took off my shoes, and tiptoed into the bathroom. I didn't want to have to re-clean it after working so hard on it the first time. Bundling my clothes into the hamper, so mud didn't get all over the floor, I turned the shower on as hot as I could stand it, and got in. As the water ran down over my body, I thought about all the jobs I had to do because I hit Harvey. All I had to do was remember the things he said to me and the way he said them, and I knew it had been worth it.

After getting cleaned up and putting my muddy clothes in the wash, I went for a walk. I wanted to be by myself so no one could bother me. A rock lay in my path, and I kicked it as hard as I could. I wanted to go home and have things back the way they were. At home I had friends, things to do, people who loved me. Here, I had nothing. I didn't fit in. I felt a burning at the back of my throat like the tears I had been trying to avoid all day were going to catch up to me.

I ran alongside the fence of the pasture, then past the barn out to the stream. Once I started, I didn't seem to be able to stop. I ran alongside of the stream until I reached the clearing in the woods. My chest ached and heaved with each short, raspy breath. My heart seemed to pound in my ears, and sweat trickled down my forehead. Looking out past the stream, I leaned against a tree and slowly slid to the ground.

I missed my Daddy. I missed the strength of his arms hugging me, comforting me. Why was this happening? I should have known he was sick, why didn't I see it? Picking up some nearby rocks, I threw them into the stream. Angry with myself for not noticing the illness, angry with Daddy for not telling me sooner, and most of all angry with God for making Daddy sick. I got up and walked through the woods. Homesick, angry, sad, and scared, how could I be feeling so many things all at once? I stayed out walking for a long time, and didn't notice how dark it had grown. I went back to the house as quickly as I could. The porch light was shining in the darkness, and Sarah stood in the doorway looking out.

Her body looked tense, but when she saw me coming, she relaxed. "Where have you been? I've been worried sick about you."

"I was just out walking around." Did I have to tell her everything I did? "I don't want to talk about it." I walked straight past her and into the house. I didn't stop to talk to anyone, but kept going until I reached my room, and flopped down on the bed. It was hard to say what I was feeling. Angry, hurt, lonely.

A couple of minutes later Sarah came in and sat beside me. "Katie honey, I can tell you're upset about something."

I scowled up at her.

"I know you don't want to talk about it now. When you do feel like talking, I'll be ready to listen." She stroked my hair as she spoke. "It's not good to keep things bottled up inside."

I wanted to throw my arms around her and sob. She patted my hand and got up to leave. I quickly sat up. "Don't go yet." I couldn't explain it. I didn't want to talk, but I didn't want to be alone either. I wanted to be held, but couldn't ask that. Sarah sat down again with her back against the headrest. When I moved next to her, she put her arm around me and gave me a squeeze. Then, she quietly hummed.

Tears stung the back of my eyelids and I tried to fight them back. One by one they welled up, flowing over the edge, and made silent, salty tracks down my cheeks. I raised my hand and brushed them away. I was grateful to Sarah for pretending not to notice. She kept humming and stroking my hair, staring at the wall but not really looking at anything.

I took a deep breath, swallowed hard, and managed to stop the flow. "Sarah? Why doesn't my Daddy want me to be with him?"

She turned her head for the first time and looked straight into my eyes. She paused for a moment before answering. "Honey, your Daddy loves you, but he can't have you at the hospital with him." She took a deep breath. "You're not here because he doesn't want you." The tears started falling again. She answered the question I was afraid to ask. That maybe he was too sick to want me anymore. "He wants the best for you."

That's what he told me right before he put me on the bus. "How am I supposed to know if that's true?" A sob started to choke me. No one told me why this was supposed to be the best for me. As far as I was concerned, the best for me was to be with my Daddy, and not to be so very far away.

"How does your Daddy feel about the truth?"

The question surprised me so much that I was able to regain a little control. "He's a real stickler for it." I told him a lie once, and he nearly beat the tail end off me. He wanted to make sure there wasn't anything I'd think was worth telling a lie about.

She raised her eyebrows. "Well then?"

I glanced away. "He would tell me the truth." I paused for a moment. "I really goofed up right before he sent me here. It bothers me that I left on such a bad note. I wouldn't even tell him good-bye."

Sarah patted my leg. "Sweetie, whatever you did doesn't change your Daddy's love for you. It's unconditional." She looked down into her lap. "You've had a few very tough days, and there may be more ahead. The only thing I can tell you is that we will be here for you to help you get through it." She looked back up. "Now, I saved some supper. All we have to do is heat it up."

"No thanks, I'm not hungry." It surprised me that she didn't tell me I had to eat. "If you don't need me to clear up or anything, I'll sit here for awhile and read or something."

She got up. "All right. If you need to talk any more, about anything, let me know."

"Sarah?" She paused and turned at the door. I gave a brief smile. "Thanks."

When Sarah left, the door didn't shut all the way. I grabbed my book and leaned back, settling myself against my pillow. Opening the pages, I tried to absorb myself in the story and forget the pain in my heart. Through the open door I heard voices in the next room, and my ears pricked up when I heard my name.

"Uncle Charley, we have one very upset young girl in the next room." Great. Now she would tell all about my crying scene. Just when I thought I might be able to trust her. "I think Katie needs to see Uncle Sam." I put down the book. I definitely wanted to hear this conversation. "Right now, she's scared, lonely, feeling a little guilty and angry because she feels like she's lost control of her life." Sarah seemed to understand my feelings, even better than I did.

"Sarah's right, Dad." Mark took my side again. "I would want to be there if I were Katie."

"Now hold on a minute." I hoped Uncle Charley would listen to them. I was ready to leave now. "Sam's in the hospital right now having tests, which should be finished up tomorrow and then he will be coming here." I could see my Daddy tomorrow. I could wait that long. "Even if we took Katie to the hospital, she wouldn't be able to see him for more than five minutes." Uncle Charley cleared his throat. "Sam doesn't want Katie to see him in the hospital."

"Dad, don't you think his judgment might be a little off?"

"No, I don't, Matthew." His voice sounded sharp, almost angry. "Sam has always put Katie first, and I don't see why that would change."

"But Uncle Sam doesn't know how much that girl is hurting." They stopped talking for a minute after Sarah said that and I could hear a chair scraping on the wooden floor.

"Let me explain something to all of you." Uncle Charley sounded somber now. "From the time Marie died, Sam's whole life has been wrapped up in Katie. He would do anything to protect her and spare her from pain. They have as close a relationship as any two people I know, and if she is feeling pain, he knows it and feels it too."

That was true. Daddy and I had always been very close. Even with my recent restlessness. It was silent in the next room except for the scratching of the chairs on the floor as someone moved. Sarah broke the silence first. "I have things to get ready for the picnic tomorrow."

I grabbed my book and tried to bury myself in the story again. After reading for awhile, my eyes, heavy with sleep, refused to stay open. I turned out the light and went to sleep.

Sweet Revenge

I woke up early in order to get all of my chores out of the way as soon as possible. The morning held the promise of a beautiful day. I looked forward to the picnic because it was one of the town's major events of the year, and it would give me a chance to see Tom. Plus, I tried not to get my hopes up too high, but I might get to see my Daddy again today.

By the time I returned to the house, Sarah had breakfast started. "I'm glad you're up early. We have a lot to do. I laid a dress out on the bed for you to put on later."

"Dress? I'm not going to wear a dress to a picnic." We weren't going to church or anything like that. "I thought I'd wear my jeans."

"I just meant a summer dress. I want you to look nice." There were other ways to look nice than wearing a dress. "You're not going in jeans." I frowned. I wasn't wearing a dress either. Her eyes got a mischievous glint. "I know that you'll want to wear something that'll make a good impression on the guys at the picnic." She smiled. "We'll look in your closet and pick out something we can both agree on."

What a relief. I wanted to make sure that I didn't show up in something that looked stupid. I gathered up baskets, blankets, and anything else we might need that Sarah could think of. Matt came out with his clipboard and sat down at the table. "What're you doing?"

"I'm working on the sign-up sheets and schedule for the boat race."

I walked up behind him and looked over his shoulder. "What kind of schedule do you have to make out?"

"A schedule of the heats."

"Are you going to have age divisions, or is everybody racing for the best time?"

"There are three age divisions." He turned his head to look at me. "How come you're so interested in this?"

"I thought I might compete."

A smile started to cross his face. "You?" He laughed.

"What's wrong with that?" I didn't think it was funny.

"Katie, this is a race for strength and stamina."

"So? Is there any rule that says a girl can't sign up for the race?"

Matt looked troubled. "No, but you have to have a partner, and I don't think that'll be an easy job because most of the people who are competing already have partners. They've been practicing together all summer."

I didn't think I would have as much trouble as he made out. "If I find someone can I be in the race?"

"Sure. Just don't count on finding anyone."

"Just don't be surprised when I enter."

He shrugged. "Suit yourself."

I would. I'd show him by trying to win too. Uncle Charley came out with a handful of numbered cloth squares and was looking at a piece of paper. I peered around his arm. It looked like he was holding a map of the park by the lake. "What's that for, Uncle Charley?"

"It's the map for the obstacle course. I have to go over early and lay it out."

"Can I go with you?"

He patted my shoulder. "No. You stay with Sarah and get everything else ready to bring over."

Stuck at home again. This was my chance to meet most of the kids before school next week, and I didn't want to waste a moment. "All right." I looked at the floor.

"Don't worry too much. Sarah has to be there early to set up her booth." I'd almost forgotten. I smiled up at him. "You sure change moods fast, don't you." He looked around the room. "Isn't Mark up yet?"

"I called him when I got up, but he just rolled over and went back to sleep." Matt turned back to his schedules.

Uncle Charley put his hand on my shoulder. "Katie, why don't you go pound on the door and tell him that as soon as we have eaten, Matt and I are going to leave. With or without him."

I walked along the dark hall toward the back bedroom. Just as I got to the door, Mark came flying out, still putting his shirt on and nearly knocked me over. "Hey, watch where you're going."

He stopped and finished tucking in his shirt. "Sorry Kit-Kat. I didn't know you were there." He grinned. "I'm a little behind today. Matt and I have to help Dad set up."

"You'd better hurry. Uncle Charley sent me back here to get you."

It seemed like we would never get everything ready and get out of the house. Sarah always had one last thing or another to do. Whatever it was brought something fresh to mind. At long last we were ready, and I could hardly contain my excitement as we pulled out of the drive.

Sarah glanced over at me. "What has you so wound up today? You haven't stopped moving since you got up this morning."

"I don't know. I guess it's because this is the first town picnic I've ever been to."

"You never went to any of these with your Daddy?" She seemed surprised.

"Well, we had get-togethers, but nothing this big."

When we arrived several men were putting up booths and setting up tables all over the place. Uncle Charley stood on the top of the hill waving his arms at something on the other side. When Sarah parked, I grabbed what I could from the truck and started walking. My arms felt like they were going to break before Sarah called out that I had gone far enough. Thankfully, I put everything down on the ground.

Sarah stopped right behind me. "I couldn't carry the juice jugs. Will you please go get them?"

"Sure." One more thing to break my arms with. The juice was in two, 3-gallon containers and I had to stop several times to give my arms a rest. Besides that they were so full that they kept sloshing over the side.

"Can I give you a hand?" Tom came up behind me.

"Grab one."

"Yes ma'am." He gave a mock salute before bending down to grab the handle of the jug. "What contests are you going to enter?"

"Any that I have time for and that I'm allowed to be in." Because I wasn't paying attention to the way I carried the jug, it swung out to the side, and then came back and hit me on the back of the knee. I winced and tried to keep from falling down. I put the jug down fast, so I could give the pain in my leg a chance to stop.

"Having some trouble?"

"A little bit. Give me a sec and I'll be fine."

Tom set his jug down beside mine. "You sure would look nice if you didn't have punch spilled all over you."

"Where!" I quickly searched my clothes for any stains. I thought I managed to get any that spilled on the grass.

Tom started laughing. "You should have seen your face."

"Ha, ha." But he did say I looked nice, in a kind of backhanded way. If it got Tom's attention, I was glad Sarah and I had finally agreed on a pair of light blue overalls and a pink and blue plaid blouse.

"Do you have a partner yet for the three-legged race?"

This sounded hopeful. "No, do you?"

He picked up his jug again. "I do, now." I heard Sarah calling me, and hastily grabbed my jug and started walking again.

"Are you going to be in the boat race?" I tried not to sound too interested. If he said he already had a partner, then that would be the end of it. I would have to cheer him on from the sidelines.

"I had planned to sign up, but the guy who was going to be my partner broke his arm during football camp this summer. He's still doing physical therapy to get his strength back."

Now came the tricky part, getting him to ask me to be his partner, without making it obvious. "I talked to Matt this morning, and he told me that I could sign up, but I had to find a partner too. Do you know if I have to have another girl for a partner?"

"I don't think so. Most girls don't want to compete in the race." Looks like I made a mistake by wanting to compete. "But that seems kind of silly to me. It is a lot of hard work, but we have some girls around here that can kick butt if they want to." Things were looking up. "We could row together if you want to."

Wanted to. That's what I'd been hoping for. "Sure. I think it'd be great."

Sarah had our stuff laid out on one of the tables, so Tom and I lugged the jugs over and put them on top of it. We'd brought enough food to feed an army. It looked really good too.

After setting the jug down, Tom hesitated. "I have to go help put up some booths. Where are you going to be a little bit later?"

"I don't know, probably somewhere around here." I knew where I'd be, at hard labor with Sarah giving out the orders. "Sarah has some booth that she's in charge of. If I'm not here, I'll be helping her with that."

"All right. I'll see you around."

I watched him until he joined the men moving boards around. I'd rather go help him than be stuck here, but I knew that I wouldn't be allowed to go until later.

We had a nice table shaded by a tree and overlooking the lake. I could see almost everything that was going on from our place. Everything was a mess when we arrived, but now it looked like a kind of carnival. It didn't seem long before people started arriving carrying all sorts of things.

While arranging the food in some order, I glanced across at Sarah working at her booth. I saw a big man in uniform walk up behind her and put his arms around her waist. She gave a slight jump and turned around. Then, she flung her arms around his neck and kissed him. I felt a little surprised. Sarah didn't tell me she had a boyfriend. Of course, I hadn't exactly given her the chance to confide in me. The man started moving things around in the booth.

Sarah motioned for me to join her. "Katie, I'd like you to meet my boyfriend, Jim Baines."

"Hello, Katie." He smiled and stretched out his hand.

"Hi." He certainly had a firm grip.

"Jim works for the sheriff's department here in town."

That explained the uniform. His light brown hair was cut short, and his uniform fit well over his muscular body. He wasn't as tall as my cousins, but he and Sarah looked good together, like a matched set.

He took Sarah's hand and caressed it. "I need to see your Uncle about something; do you know where he is?"

"He's on the other side of the hill setting up the obstacle course."

Jim whipped his mirrored sunglasses out of his breast pocket and covered up his gray eyes. "Will you stop back by before you leave?" Sarah sounded a little anxious.

"Of course I will, Sarah." He leaned over and gave her a quick peck on the cheek before going to talk to Uncle Charley.

I waited until he was out of hearing. "He's cute, Sarah. Where'd you find him?"

Her cheeks flushed a little before she answered. "Jim was a couple years ahead of me in high school. I always had the most terrific crush on him."

It looked like she still did. "Do you love him?"

She smiled and nodded. "Now, help me sort out these prizes. They all came jumbled together." Sarah had the baseball throw booth, and all the little plastic animals, false teeth, and other prizes for knocking down the cans were thrown into a big box, and looked hopelessly tangled. It took me a few moments to figure out what all the prizes were. The only things that separated easily were the little stuffed animals for the grand prizes.

"Hello, Sarah. How are you this morning?"

I looked quickly around. A girl about my age stood there with her hands clasped behind her back. She wore a lightweight sundress with sandals so white, they looked brand new. Her long, black hair was held back with a ribbon that was tied in a bow on the top of her head.

"Hello, Emma."

"Who is the little friend helping you with the booth today?"

Little friend? Her voice was so sweet it about made me sick. Besides, I was taller than Emma. Who did she think she was anyway? She reminded me of some kind of 'little miss perfect'.

"This is my cousin, Katie."

"Hi." This had to be the worst part about introductions. You were forced to talk to people you didn't want to be caught dead near.

"How do you do, Katie? I'm Emma Carter." She nodded her head as she spoke, and her hair bounced on her shoulders with each bob of the head.

"I'm fine." What else could I say? Sarah looked at me in a strange kind of way. I think she wanted me to try harder to keep the conversation going. "Are you entered in any of the events today Emma?"

"Oh, of course." She gave a fake little laugh. "I have my lemon chiffon cake entered in the junior bake-off." It probably tasted like sawdust. A bake-off wasn't exactly the type of contest I was talking about either. "What do you have entered?"

The only things I baked came pre-packaged at the grocery store. Was it law around here that every girl had to have something entered in the baking contest? Sarah came to my rescue. "She just got into town two days ago, Emma."

"Then you didn't have a chance to prepare anything. I'm sure you'll enter next year." As if I'd think of nothing else for that year. If I had my way, I wouldn't even be here. "If you bake anything like Sarah, you'll give me stiff competition. She makes the best pies and cakes I've ever eaten."

Obviously she was trying to butter Sarah up, but I couldn't figure out why she wanted to. "It was nice talking to you, Emma." The words almost stuck in my throat. "But I have to help Sarah out with this booth. Maybe we can talk later."

After about six or seven years on a deserted island with no one else around, I might even welcome Emma as someone I could talk to. But not until then.

Emma fluffed her hair. "I hope we'll see one another later today. Then we can sit down and have a really nice chat."

That would certainly put a damper on my afternoon. She spun quickly around to make her skirt twirl out, and her hair bounced up and down with every step. "Is she like that all the time?"

Sarah shrugged. "She is around me. Why?"

She always had to ask a question. What I really wanted to know was how she could stand Emma. But, I didn't think that would go over too well. "She sounded a little fake to me. Like she was putting up a front or something."

Sarah nodded thoughtfully. "I thought there was something you didn't like."

No kidding. Try everything.

"That's the way she is. You just have to accept her as that."

I wondered if she really believed that. From what I knew of Sarah, I didn't think she would be taken in by such phoniness. But sometimes adults were blind in the oddest things.

She handed me a basket of sorted prizes. "I don't expect you two to become best friends." Thank goodness for small favors. Touching my shoulder, she looked straight into my eyes. "All I ask is that you be civil."

She might as well ask for the moon. People were milling all over the place. The official opening of the picnic couldn't be far off. "Can I go look around for a bit?" Maybe I could find Tom and watch him work for awhile.

Sarah looked at her watch. "I want you back here in half an hour. Matt and Mark should be coming back about then too."

"Thanks."

As I walked off, I saw Uncle Charley and Jim Baines coming over the top of the hill. Motioning with his hands, Uncle Charley looked at the ground. They seemed to be deep in discussion. Just past the hill on the lake side, I thought I saw Tom. I made straight for the path around the lake.

I took my eyes off Tom long enough to look at the path and my heart nearly stopped. Harvey was setting up a lawn chair right next to the path. If I passed him, I might have to stop and talk to him, and I couldn't think of anything I'd rather do less. I took the scenic route over the top if the hill so there wouldn't be any chance that he would talk to me. I couldn't avoid him forever, but any time I could spend away from him was better than nothing. I started down the hill when I heard my name being called.

Shoot. "Katie!" I stopped but didn't turn around. Who was calling me now? "Hey Kit-Kat, I need a little help. Come here." As I turned I saw Mark holding up some tangled rope.

"All right. Just remember this when I need a favor." It really wasn't all that tangled, it just took two people to undo it. "Now that that's taken care of what do we do with it?"

Mark grinned. "I'm glad you asked that."

Uh-oh. Why did I have to open my big mouth? I'd be stuck helping out longer than I thought and it would be time to go back by the time we finished.

"The rope needs to be laid out as a boundary for the obstacle course."

My time was running out too. I had to be back in less than fifteen minutes, and I hadn't even talked to Tom. "Where's Uncle Charley? I thought he was supposed to be doing this?"

Mark tossed the rope at me. "He's busy with something else right now. Take your end and tie it to that pylon over there." He pointed clear across the hill.

"What are you going to do?"

"After you get your end tied down, I'll tie down this one."

Great. I got to walk all the way there and back again and he would just stand there. It figured that I would have to do all the leg work. "Don't overwork yourself."

By the time I got through helping Mark it was time to go back.

"Matt and I have to watch a couple of the contests. If I can sneak away from them for a little while, how'd you like to be my partner for the piggy-back races?"

I pretended to think about it for a moment. "I don't know. You might not have enough energy after all the work you've done this morning."

"Very funny."

Matt made it back to the table before we did. Sarah didn't even give me a chance to sit down before she started in on me. "It's about time you got back. What took you so long?"

Questions. Too many questions. Daddy didn't want to know where I was this much.

"The rope was tangled and we had to get it sorted out. I saw Katie and asked her to help me with it." Thank goodness Mark answered and not me. I wouldn't have been that nice.

"Hey Matt! You can put my name down for the boat race."

He raised his eyebrows. "Do you have a partner?"

"Tom Pike."

Matt picked up his clipboard and wrote the name down. "You're sure you want to do this?"

"Why not?"

He shrugged. "Just don't complain to me tomorrow that your arms hurt."

We sat down to eat, but Uncle Charley hadn't come back yet. Sarah said that he wanted us to start without him, and he would be there as soon as possible. As soon as we finished eating, I ran off to find Tom so we could start winning contests. We came in second in the three-legged race. It felt great to have his arm around my waist as we ran toward the finish line.

The only thing that stopped us from winning was the fact that my legs were shorter than his and it tripped us up twice. Once we got into the swing of things though, nothing could have stopped us. If we had had a chance to practice a bit more before the start of the race, we would have won.

We stopped by Tom's table for something to drink after the race. The heat of the day made me very thirsty. For some reason, I only wanted water, not punch or pop.

Tom put his hand on my shoulder. "Cheer up." Cheer up? I wasn't sad. "Next time Ted gets in front of us like that, I'll tie his shoelaces together."

I smiled. "I don't think his partner would've been too happy when he tripped and brought her down with him."

Tom put his cup down. "You're right. Debbi wouldn't have found it very funny."

We started walking along the path. I couldn't believe it, Tom knew everyone at the picnic. Every time we passed someone, he waved and had something to say.

"So. When are you going to introduce me to all your friends?"

He looked around. "Who? The people I've been talking to?" I nodded. "They're just people I know. Not really friends of mine." He sure seemed to know a lot about them. "Mike and Pete are the guys I hang around with the most. You already know them."

I had met them. That didn't mean I knew them. But then again, I hadn't known Tom for very long either, and we seemed to be hitting it off just fine. "Do you have any girls you hang around with?" I gave him a mock innocent look. "Or don't you like girls?" I wanted to know whether I had any competition.

He glanced at me sideways. "You're wicked."

A slow smile crept across my face. "I just want to make sure that you don't have a girlfriend stashed away somewhere."

He laughed. "Well, judging by the bruises on the face of your last boyfriend, I certainly don't want to get on your wrong side." I shot him a look of outrage. "Have you seen Harvey's face today? It's black and blue."

Great. I avoided him earlier because I didn't want to know if his jaw still hurt or not. I wanted to wait until enough time had passed so it would only be a memory. Not something the whole world could see. "Harvey, for your information, falls into the category of the last person on the face of the earth who I would have for a boyfriend. I've been trying to stay away from him."

"Why?"

I raised one shoulder in a half-shrug. "I didn't think he'd be very nice. I got into enough trouble for hitting him and I don't want it to happen again." And the whole incident embarrassed me horribly. I wanted to forget it ever happened.

"Katie." Mark signaled me from the top of the hill.

"Will you have to go do something else now?" Tom sounded concerned that I might leave him, and that made me feel good inside.

"I don't think so. I promised Mark that I'd be his rider for the piggy-back race." Tom slipped his hand in mine and we started climbing the hill hand in hand. "Will you stay and cheer us on?"

"Are you kidding? I wouldn't miss this for the world."

When we got to the top, Mark held his hand out to Tom. "Hey Tom. It's been awhile since I've seen you. How are things going?"

Tom dropped my hand to shake Mark's. "I'm doing great. You should have seen Katie and me in the three-legged race. I'd have won if she would've stood up for half of it." He and Mark laughed. I stared at him and tapped my foot on the ground waiting. "What? Did I say something wrong?" He looked at me with pretended innocence like I had wounded him somehow.

"I could always say the same about you, you know." I mimicked his innocent look right back at him.

Mark ran a hand through his dark hair. "That must have been some race to see."

"It was." I made my voice as sarcastic as I could. "For all my clumsiness, we still came in second."

"Well, Kit-Kat, are you ready to triumph in the piggy-back race?" Mark rubbed his hands together.

"Of course." I was always ready to win. I never started out to lose in anything.

Tom leaned over and whispered in my ear. "He calls you Kit-

Kat?" I shrugged. It was not something I could explain.

Mark knelt down at the starting line. Tom left us to go stand by the finish line. I almost laughed out loud when I saw H.L. Denton. He had on what had to be his 'Western Wear', a plaid shirt, blue jeans tucked into boots, a kerchief tied around his neck, and a cowboy hat topped everything off. Being the official starter of the race, he even had a holster for the starter gun.

"Riders mount up."

I climbed on Mark's back and he stood up. "Am I in a comfortable spot for you?"

"You're a little high. See if you can slide down a bit." He grabbed ahold of my legs as I slid down his back. "There. That's perfect."

"Where do you want my arms to be?"

He shifted my position a little bit more. "Hold on to my shoulders. And lean forward while I'm running." He walked over to our lane. "If you lean back it'll slow me down because it throws my balance off."

I looked down the line and saw Matt with Sarah as his rider. I didn't know they would be in the race too. Sarah saw me and waved.

Before I had a chance to tell Mark they were there, Matt turned and yelled at us. "Hey Mark! You two are going to eat our dust."

"No way! By the time you cross the starting line, we'll be halfway home." Mark stepped across the line to face him. "Let's say we make a little wager on it."

Matt walked over to the lane beside us. "You're on. Loser pays ten bucks."

"It's a bet."

H.L. called the racers to order, raised his pistol, and slowly pulled the trigger. As soon as he heard the bang, Mark took off running. I leaned forward and tried to stay as close to him as I could because I didn't want to take the blame if he lost. He and Matt ran neck and neck most of the way. It almost seemed as if they were the only two in the race because everyone else was so far behind.

At the very end of the race, Mark seemed to find an extra bit of energy. When I didn't think he could run any faster, we seemed to fly over the finish line, split seconds before Matt and Sarah. He came to a stop and let me slide off his back. He walked over to Matt and slapped him on the arm. "Good race." He held out his hand. "Now pay up."

Sarah shook her head. "I don't know about you guys. One of these days you're going to kill yourselves trying to outdo one another."

While they continued talking, I slipped away with Tom. "Oh no." I stopped walking.

"What's wrong?"

"I have to go back. I forgot to ask when it's our turn to do the row boat thing."

Tom took my hand and started walking forward again. "That's all right. I already checked with Matt. We're in the second to the last heat." Trust Matt to make us wait until the last part of the day when we'd be all tired out. We wouldn't have as good of a chance to win. "What's wrong now?"

I must have been scowling. "I just hoped we'd be able to go sooner than that. It's nothing."

"You're not looking at it right. We've got one of the best heats there are."

I stopped dead. "What?"

Tom rolled his eyes toward the sky. "Look. By going second to the last, we know who we have to beat. We'll have a general idea of how fast everyone is going." That made sense. "Don't look now, but Harvey's headed this way, and he's got Emma with him." From the way he said Emma's name, I got the feeling that Tom didn't like her any more than I did. "Do you want to go the other way? Since we're stopped we can pretend we were headed another direction to begin with."

"No. I have to face him sometime. It might as well be now, while I have one of my Musketeers with me." I turned around to wait for the inevitable. I decided that things might not go so bad if I got the first words in. I forced myself to smile. "Hi there, Harvey. Hi, Emma."

"Hi yourself." Was this the same girl who had been so sickeningly sweet to me this morning? Instead of being prissily over polite, she was downright rude and obnoxious. It was probably more in tune with her true character. "Hi, Tom. Just in case you're interested, I have a lemon chiffon cake entered in the baking contest. You should get yourself a piece after the judging is over." There was the sickening girl I met earlier.

One thing that seemed strange was that Harvey's face didn't look nearly as bad as I remembered it. Maybe in the excitement of hitting him, it looked worse than it was. I somehow expected it to still be swollen and distorted. I had let go of Tom's hand in case I had to shake hands with them, however disgusting that would have been. Now they just hung at my sides and it felt awkward not having anything to do with them.

"I heard that you and Katie are going to be a team for the row boats." Harvey talked to Tom as if I wasn't there, and his voice sounded as repulsive as ever.

"Can't you just imagine Katie in a row boat? How ridiculous." Emma snickered and laid her hand on Harvey's arm.

I bit the end of my tongue. I wanted to tell her off in the worst way, but I knew if I did, she'd get me in trouble somehow. I took a deep breath to calm myself. "Ridiculous? I'm surprised that you and Harvey aren't going to be a team." How cool I sounded.

Emma flushed and bit her lip. "Trying to compete with the boys is vulgar." Her voice sneered with every word.

I wanted to say something to get under her skin, but not anything that she could take hold of. I had to maintain my coolness. "I'm sorry. I forgot." I put as much pity into my voice as I could. "Little girls don't always understand that playing with boys is a way of life. Maybe you'll learn how when you grow up."

Her face turned bright red, and she couldn't talk because she was so angry. Her mouth snapped open and shut so many times, she looked like a fish trying to get some air. Out of the corner of my eye, I saw Tom's hand fly up to his mouth to keep him from laughing out loud.

"Well, I never!"

"That's right. And you probably never will."

Emma stomped off with Harvey following her like a puppy dog. What an absolutely perfect couple.

"I can't believe how you handled that." Tom's grin spread clear across his face. "I was right when I called you wicked." I would take that as a compliment. "I thought for a minute you were going to lose it."

"I almost did, but this was better." I laughed. "That felt so good. I stayed in control and chewed her out at the same time."

"When did you meet Emma? You haven't been in town for too long and she isn't exactly the social butterfly she likes to think she is."

"She trapped me over at the baseball throw booth." Even remembering it made me shudder. "She was wearing her phony 'nice' face around Sarah." I paused for a moment. "I think Emma likes you."

He gave a slight start. "What?" His surprise seemed genuine. "Where did you get that from? That's an awful place in my head now."

I shrugged. "I don't know. It just seemed like it to me."

"She does try to impress me sometimes, but it makes me sick." That's what I thought. "What a nightmare of a thought, Emma after me."

"You mean I don't have to be jealous that she was trying to tempt you with lemon chiffon?"

Tom laughed. "No worries there."

We walked down by the lake. There were some kids in shorts and rolled up pants splashing along the shore. Some others had suits on and were swimming out to the float and diving off the edge. As we stood watching all the people, Tom slipped his arm across my shoulders. It startled me, and I gave a slight jump. He quickly put his arm down at his side.

"This school year's gonna be great. You and Emma are going to be the best of friends. I can tell already." His voice sounded forced and the words were rushed, like he was trying to cover up his embarrassment.

My cheeks burned. I hadn't meant to jump. It was just so

unexpected. It felt nice, and I didn't mind his arm around me, but I couldn't tell him that. I'd just have to wait for him to work up his courage again and hope that I'd be ready.

Tom looked at his watch. "It's almost time for our race. Let's go see about a boat and some oars." We picked out a nice boat that had cushions on the seats. The day was so nice; I almost wished we weren't entered in the race so we could take a leisurely row around the lake. "What we need to do is get a rhythm going and keep it up." He tossed me an oar. "We won't go anywhere unless we pull together."

The boats had to stay half on shore and one member of the team had to push it off and then jump in. Tom volunteered to do that for us. We had the outside starting position. We got off to a great start. We seemed to glide through the water. As we approached a nice shady cove to our left, I saw a boat coming out of it, angled to cross our bow and cut us off. "Tom! To our left."

"What?" His head snapped around to look. "Try to out run them."

I didn't see how we could. The boat was ahead of us, and going faster would make us crash into it. I turned my head to get a better look. Harvey and Emma. I kept pulling as hard as I could, hoping against hope that we would outdistance them. My arms could definitely feel the burn. If they cut us off, we would lose the race for sure. I knew they had hidden in the cove waiting for us to pass so they could make us lose. The boats collided and the jolt sent me flying forward out of my seat. I heard jeering laughter from the other boat.

"What in the world do you think you're doing?" I'd never heard Tom yell like that before. He sounded furious.

"We're sorry. We didn't mean to bump into you." Not only did the words sound fake, but when I picked myself up from the bottom of the boat, Harvey had a smug smile on his bruised face.

"I guess it doesn't pay to have a girl for a partner in these kinds of races, does it Tom?" Emma's words were dripping with acid honey. "She gets you into wrecks and you lose the race."

"Since you're in a rowboat Emma, you shouldn't talk so high and mighty." My temper was definitely rising. "As I recall, you're the one who said that girls in rowboats were ridiculous." I spat the words out of my mouth. "And I think you used the word vulgar."

Emma stood up. "How dare you!" Her voice shrill, she took a step forward.

"I only used your words." And they were great weapons. As she took another step forward, I pushed the side of their boat down and away as hard as I could. Emma lost her balance and started to go over the edge. She probably would have fallen to the bottom of the boat if Harvey hadn't stood up too. The boat rocked so hard that it threw her up against the side. As she went over, she clutched at Harvey and pulled him into the lake with her.

When she came up, her face was the picture of fury. They both looked exactly like what they were, a couple of drowned rats. Tom and I laughed so hard, we almost split our sides. Harvey kept yelling at us, but we couldn't understand what he said.

Every time one of them tried to climb into the boat, the other tried from the other side. The boat kept bobbing up and down, and they lost their hold and fell into the lake again.

Harvey swam over to our boat and was going to try and climb up. Tom waited until he kicked up to reach for the edge and then with the paddle end of the oar pushed Harvey in the chest. Harvey went under and Tom kept him from surfacing for a few seconds by holding the oar on the top of his head. "Start rowing."

I quickly grabbed my oars and started to row. A sharp tug almost wrenched an oar from my grasp. I had forgotten about Emma while watching Tom and Harvey scuffle. Since she still had a hold of the oar, I gave it a big push. It accidentally hit her in the face. She went under. I held my breath. A couple of seconds later she came back up sputtering. I breathed a sigh of relief and began to row as hard as I could.

When Tom and I left them, they were trying to get back into their boat. Laughing, I grabbed Tom's arm. "Well? Did that make up for not winning the race?"

Tom's eyes twinkled. "I think it might do. I'll treasure the memory of the two of them bobbing up and down with the boat." He brushed his hair back. "They looked as stupid as 'Beach Bobbing Bob' when he falls into the water."

My head snapped back in confusion. "Who?"

"It's a stupid online game where you have to get Bob, a monkey, to leap across the water, jumping on barrels to bring coconuts from one side of the water to the other. Sometimes the barrels sink or blow up and Bob ends up getting dunked." He laughed again. "We also just got even with Harvey for the stunt he pulled the other day by sticking us with the check."

We explained to Matt what happened and he marked us down as a disabled boat. With Tom as a witness maybe I wouldn't get in trouble if Emma showed up with bruises. Matt stopped us as we started to leave. "Sarah's been looking for you. She says it's time to start packing things up."

As I turned to head in that direction, I saw Uncle Charley talking to Sarah. That gave me a few extra minutes to spend with Tom. I stopped underneath the shade of a tree. "I had a great time today."

Tom nodded, but seemed a little distracted.

I shrugged. "I probably should go before Sarah sends out a search party." I wondered if I had done something to make him not like me. "I can't believe I have to go already."

Half turned to go, I took a step forward. Tom grabbed my arms and swung me around toward him. He pulled me in close and kissed me quickly on the lips. "Today was special because of you." He kissed me again, longer and more intimately. He let go of my arms and stepped back. "I'll see you at school." He turned and ran off.

My mouth still tingled from his kiss. I slowly walked over to our table, a warm cozy feeling spreading through my body.

Going Home

After packing up all the things from the picnic, Sarah and I got into her truck to go home. Tired as I was, my mind kept racing with thoughts of the day. "I had so much fun. Today was just great." The best part was my first kiss, but I wasn't ready to share that yet. "Don't you think so?" Sarah kept driving as if she hadn't heard me. "Sarah?" Still no reaction. "Sarah." I raised my voice to get her attention.

She briefly turned her head. "What?"

"Wasn't today fun? I had such a good time."

"Yes." She didn't even sound sure about it. Her hands clenched the steering wheel.

I kept trying to figure out if I had done anything wrong. I didn't think so, unless she was upset about Harvey and Emma getting dumped into the lake. If that was bothering her though, she would have jumped on me for it right away. She wouldn't wait until we got home. No, it had to be something worse than that.

Her profile was rigid and her teeth were clenched as if she was holding something back. I wanted to do something to help in some way, but I didn't know what to say. I felt awkward about saying anything, but I felt I had to try. After all, she helped me feel better when I was feeling homesick.

I couldn't say the right thing if I didn't know what was wrong. "Sarah? If it's something I said or did." My voice trailed off as she bit her lip and shook her head. Tears started trickling down her cheeks. "I'm sorry." This was exactly what I wanted to avoid. "I didn't mean to upset you." Whatever happened must have been bad. Worse than I thought and here I was sticking my foot in my mouth. "Is there anything I can do?"

"No." The word barely came out. She took a deep breath. "Honey, just be quiet until we get home." She said it softly with a shaky voice.

I began to wonder if maybe Jim broke up with her, although it didn't look that way when I saw him with her. Fortunately, the house was only a couple of minutes away. Maybe when we got home, I could bring in all the dishes and baskets and put them away, without being asked. I didn't know how else to help.

When we arrived at the house, Sarah went straight into the bathroom. I heard her turn on the water and fill up the sink. I quickly carried in everything from the truck, and almost had it all put away when she came out again. She helped me put the rest away, and we started washing the dishes. We worked side by side in silence. She obviously didn't want to talk, and I didn't want to say anything because it might make her cry again.

I put the last dish away as Matt, Mark, and Uncle Charley drove up. They came quietly in the house, and for once, no one had a smile to give. They only looked at me through sad eyes. I began to get scared. "What is wrong with everyone? We just got back from a great picnic."

I had to get someone to smile. Panic started to fill me. "Boy this family sure is weird. Most people are happy and relaxed after a picnic."

"Katie." Uncle Charley spoke softly, but the one word seemed to pierce right through me. "Sit down. We have something to talk about."

Something was terribly wrong. He didn't look this serious when I hit Harvey. Mark put his hand on the doorknob. "I have to tend to the animals."

Uncle Charley looked at him and started to say something, but didn't. His gaze was only away from me for a second. I backed toward my chair, felt it with my hand, and sat down. Sarah came in and sat down too. Matt stood by the door tapping a pencil up and down on his clipboard, carefully not looking at me.

"Katie, I'm afraid I have some bad news." Uncle Charley's eyes looked pained.

I felt something squeezing my heart. Not Daddy. Anything but that. "If Daddy's worse, he'll want to see me." I started to get out of my chair. "I'll go pack some things or we can just leave right now."

"Katie, just hear me out." I sank slowly back into my chair. The grief in his voice was plain. I didn't want to know the rest. "He had cancer and it spread to his liver before anything could be done about it."

Had? What did he mean had?

His voice grew rough and gravelly. "The doctors did all they could." His voice broke. Sarah wept silently and Matt turned his head. My brain had been frozen, not really taking everything in, but now something snapped.

"No! I don't want to hear any more." I sprang to my feet, tears blurring my vision. "Take me home to my Daddy. I need to see him."

Uncle Charley came over and took my hands. "I'm sorry Katie. I got the call while we were at the picnic. Your Daddy died this morning in his sleep."

No. It had to be a mistake. It couldn't be my Daddy. Hot tears started sliding down my face. Daddies were supposed to be there when you grew up. My Daddy was too big and strong to give in to death. I began to sob. I wished everyone would stop looking at me. They looked as helpless as I felt, and it hurt me. Everything seemed to be happening in slow motion.

Sarah touched my shoulder. "Katie."

"No! Leave me alone!" How loud my voice sounded. I had to get out of there. I couldn't stand their watching eyes anymore.

I jerked my shoulder away from her touch, and pulled my hand back from Uncle Charley. I ran blindly toward the door, and bumped into Matthew. I pushed angrily against him, and continued out the door.

I heard Uncle Charley talking as I left. "Let her go. She needs some time alone."

Time alone. I needed my Daddy. I saw Mark coming out of the

barn, Günter at his side. I didn't want to talk to anyone. Mark leaned down and said something to Günter and as I ran toward my special place in the woods, Günter followed at my side.

I wanted to yell and scream. I wanted to hit something, break things. What would happen to me now? Abandoned, alone in the world, I was an orphan. Those people in the house were strangers. They didn't know anything about me. I had nowhere else to go.

Falling to my knees, I put my arms around Günter's neck and buried my face on his back. I cried until not another tear would fall. Sitting back against a tree, I waited for my breath to slow down, and to stop jumping in my chest. My throat felt closed like it was swollen and wouldn't let another sound pass through it.

As I sat there, thoughts of Daddy kept popping into my head. I didn't want to think about him. It hurt. But, there he was tucking me into bed, telling me a story, and then kissing me good night. His arms hugging me when I hurt myself. The stern expression on his face when I had done something wrong. Sitting on his lap in the evening, talking about our day.

Even though my nose felt stuffed up, it started running. I didn't have any Kleenex either. I crawled over to the stream and washed off my face. It made me feel a little better, but not much. I knew I had to go back to the house, but I didn't want to. I never wanted to go back. If it hadn't been for them, I could have been with my Daddy when he died. Tears welled up in my eyes again. I didn't see how I had any left.

I slowly stood up. The woods were dark, and I could barely see in front of me. With each reluctant step, I made my way toward the house. Günter stayed by my side, not running off as he usually did. I came to the edge of the woods.

I stood for a moment staring at the house from behind a tree. Everything would be different now. I'd have a new family, and I didn't want them. The porch light and the light from the half moon were the only things breaking the darkness. How cozy the house looked, and how outside and alone I felt.

How could I fit into that cheerful, white house when I felt like half of me was missing? It was full of warmth and happiness, and I was empty, and pain filled the hole. A gentle breeze was blowing, and the porch swing started creaking as it moved. With leaden feet I walked over to the swing and sat down. I couldn't bring myself to go inside yet.

After a couple minutes Uncle Charley came out and sat down beside me. He must have been watching from the window. He didn't say anything, or try to give me false comfort. We sat there swinging back and forth with no sound except the soft creaking of the swing.

I broke the silence first. "What happens now?"

He didn't say anything for a moment, just stared straight ahead. "We'll have the funeral tomorrow afternoon."

"What?" I couldn't believe they would have it so soon.

"I know it seems a little fast, but that's the way Sam wanted it. He made the arrangements when he went in the hospital." Tears sprang into Uncle Charley's eyes. "He didn't want us to have to deal with having to make the arrangements." The words barely reached my mind. Everything felt unreal. "After the funeral, we'll go back to the house and pack up all your things and bring as much as we can back with us."

I didn't want to pack up my things. I wanted to stay in my house. I didn't want to see the people I grew up with staring at me and looking sad.

"I'm your legal guardian now, and you'll always have a home with me." He patted my hand. He was trying to be nice, but all I wanted was my Daddy. Uncle Charley stood up. "You come in when you're ready."

I didn't feel like I'd ever be ready to go back into that house. My brain went numb, and I couldn't think or feel anymore. All I could do was sit and swing back and forth. The night air grew cold, and my arms started getting goose pimples. I still couldn't make myself go in the house. Sarah brought out a blanket and put it around my shoulders and then went back inside. I heard the screen door creak again.

She came back out with something hot and steamy in her hands. "I brought you some tea. I thought you might need it." She sat down beside me and wrapped my hands around the cup. I brought it to my lips and took a sip. The warmth felt good. I had been colder than I thought. As I drank my tea, we swung silently back and forth.

I bit my lower lip. I felt like I was going to cry again. The numbness started fading, and one thought ran through my head like a nightmarish song. My Daddy was dead. One salty tear followed the next down my cheeks. I gulped the tea to try and stop them from flowing.

I sat the cup down on the ground. The tears kept coming faster and faster. Sarah reached over and stroked my hair. I turned and flung my arms around her. She held me and rocked slowly to and fro. I cried myself out again.

"I'm sorry." I pulled back. I felt like I had cried more since coming to this house than I had cried in my whole life.

She looked puzzled. "What're you sorry about?"

"I didn't mean to cry anymore." I touched her shoulder. "And I got your blouse all wet."

Shaking her head, Sarah patted me on the back. "This blouse has to get washed anyway, and there's nothing wrong with tears." Her eyes turned grave. "I've shed a few myself." That's why she cried on the way home. "When I was young, I used to stay with your Daddy and Mamma a lot. They were very special to me."

She reached over and picked up the cup. "Why don't we go in before we freeze out here?" She stood up and waited. "It can be hot during the day, but once the sun goes down it gets downright chilly."

I still didn't want to go in, but I knew I couldn't spend the night on the porch swing either.

I awoke early in the morning, after a fitful night's sleep. My head ached, and my eyes felt gritty from all the crying I had done. No one said much while we were getting ready, and it wasn't long before we headed out the door.

It seemed to be such a long trip, but with every passing mile, I wished they would multiply. That way it'd take a lot longer to get there. In one way, I wanted the trip to take forever. In another, I wanted it over and done with. I didn't want to deal with what happened when the truck stopped.

Sarah drove without speaking for a while. I didn't mind because there was nothing to say. Matt's car sped along in front of us, kicking dust at our faces. Somehow that seemed right. I felt like dirt. I looked nice, but felt a little uncomfortable in my blue, white and black plaid dress. It was the only appropriate thing I had for the funeral.

Funeral. What an awful word. I couldn't remember ever having been to one before, but I supposed I had gone to my mother's. Now who was going to tell me stories about my Mamma? No one else knew her like Daddy, and I didn't know enough about her.

"How're you doing, Katie?"

If I told the truth, I was on the verge of tears again. "Hanging in there." I glanced out the window. We were getting close. I made it out this far on one of my runaway attempts. Daddy found me right after that though. He always found me. Not anymore. I wanted to come home, but didn't want it this way.

The cars rolled to a stop in front of the church. Sarah got out. "Are you coming?"

"In a minute." If I had my way, I'd sit in the truck for the whole service. I just sat there staring straight ahead trying not to think about what came next.

After a while, Uncle Charley came out of the church and over to the truck. My door opened. "It's time now Katie." My legs felt like lead as I swung them around. Each step seemed harder to take than the last. People were arriving. I didn't want anyone to talk to me. I kept looking at the ground so I wouldn't have to meet their eyes.

After the service, I couldn't remember anything that was said. I remembered stupid little things. Like Reverend Archer having a cold in his nose that made some words sound funny. Through the whole thing, I stared at a hole someone had dug in the rail in front of me. When everyone came out, we stood by the door for the people to pay their condolences. The only way I got through it was Uncle Charley keeping his hand on my shoulder. It gave me a sense of comfort.

The graveside service would come next. "Katie." Uncle Charley's voice was quiet. "Would you like to pay your last respects before we go to the cemetery?"

I numbly nodded. Last respects. How final and unyielding that sounded.

The room was almost overpowered with the smell of flowers. The dim light helped to create a sense of peace and the quiet gave me a chance to shut everything else out. I walked over to the plain pine casket. The top was closed by my Daddy's wishes. He wanted me to remember him the way he was, not laid out in fine clothes, not moving, not breathing. I rubbed my hands across the polished top. Even the wood felt cold and lifeless.

Tears gently streamed down my cheeks. Not the sobs of the day before, just simple grief. For the first time I could remember, crying didn't seem to matter. As I stood there running my hands across the top, I felt the presence of my Daddy in the room, felt his love.

"Daddy?" My voice echoed in the empty room. "If you can hear me now, I have something to tell you." I waited for a moment, half expecting to hear his voice. "Daddy. I miss you. I'll love you always." My voice started to shake, but I regained control. "Watch over me Daddy. You always said you would."

I paused again to swallow down my lump. "All I want to know is why? You mean too much to me to be dead." I hit the top of the casket and hurriedly left the room. I dried my tears before joining the others.

Now I had to face the hardest thing of all, the graveside service. I didn't want to watch men throw dirt over what used to be my Daddy. He had to be able to hear me, to know what I felt, and what I was thinking. I stood apart from the crowd and back a ways.

Matt came back and stood by me. "Wouldn't you like to move in closer Katie?"

"No." The word exploded from my lips. "I'm sorry; I didn't mean to say it that way."

Matt gave me a quick hug. "That's all right. I understand." He stood for a moment looking toward the grave. "Would you like me to stay, or would you rather be by yourself?"

I grabbed his hand. "Stay."

He gave my hand a quick squeeze, and then put his arm across my shoulders. I didn't listen to what was being said. I just looked at the people. Everyone looked strange, different somehow. Maybe I was used to seeing them in everyday clothes and acting like themselves. Timmy looked funny in his light brown suit that was two inches too short for him. His hair was neatly combed and slicked down. Something I never saw before. Mr. Pickford had on a dark blue suit. I didn't even know he owned such a thing. His shoes were polished up with a spit-polish shine. The Reverend's white socks were slowly inching down.

I heard the scraping of the shovel as it was picked up. I covered my eyes. Someone dug into the pile for a shovelful of dirt. I squeezed Matt's hand tight. There was a pause as he aimed to toss it. Then a shower of dirt hit the casket. I felt as if every lump and particle of it was hitting me and piercing through my body.

I turned toward Matt and buried my face on his chest. "Take me home, Matt. I want to go now."

He put his arms around me. "It's all right, Katie. We'll leave if you want to." He took me by the hand and led me over to the car. "Let me tell Dad that we're leaving."

I sat down in the car to wait for him. I stared straight ahead, not really seeing anything. He came back sooner than I expected. "We'll take Sarah's truck. She'll ride back with Mark."

Before long, we drove up to the house. I stayed in the truck. "Are you coming in?" Matt opened the door.

I shook my head. "Not yet. I'm not ready." A feeling deep down inside told me that this might be even harder to cope with than the service I just left. "Go ahead. I'll come in later."

He gave me one last look and went inside. I didn't want to pass through the door and have my Daddy not be there. Funeral or not, I just couldn't believe he was dead. If I walked into the house, and he wasn't there, it would be real. Final. I didn't want to be in the truck when the rest of the family arrived though. Facing people was a whole different ordeal I wanted to avoid.

I slowly unglued my legs from the seat of the truck and walked up to the door. Standing outside for a moment, I gathered my courage to open it and go in. I walked through the doorway and took a deep breath. Everything looked the same, like Daddy would be coming home any minute. A footstep sounded from his bedroom.

I had to swallow hard when I saw Matt moving around in there. He looked so much like Daddy that tears came to my eyes again. If I started crying here, I might not be able to stop. Looking around the living room, memories of all the good times we spent together came flooding back to me. I couldn't take much more, so I ran into my room.

Here I could sit in peace and quiet. Not as many memories to pester me. I sat down on the edge of my bed and stared at the wall. The room looked too neat to be mine. Daddy was always on my back to keep it cleaned up, but somehow, living in it seemed to make it cluttered. I couldn't believe I had only been gone for a few days. It seemed like forever.

Looking out my window, I tried to force all thoughts from my mind. I didn't want to think about anything. I wished I could make time stop and go backward. Maybe things would work out differently. Maybe my Daddy wouldn't have had to die.

The front door squeaked open, and I could hear the shuffle of feet. The murmur of voices came through the door. Then things got quiet, and I heard furniture being moved, and dishes being taken out of the cupboard. Someone was by the mantle taking down the pictures. I felt like my life was being torn down and packed up.

The door of my room opened, and Sarah stuck her head around the corner. "Mind if I come in?"

"No."

She came in and sat down beside me. "It was a nice service, wasn't it?" I gave a nod. How could it be a nice service? My Daddy was dead. "We need to get started in here. We don't have a lot of time to pack today." She stood up and walked over to the door. "I'm going to get a couple boxes. Why don't you start getting something ready?"

I didn't want to box anything up. This house was my last tie to my Daddy, and they wanted to tear it apart, pack it up, and sell it. When Sarah came back, I hadn't even moved. She didn't say anything, but opened up my closet and started taking out clothes. She laid them on the bed next to me.

"I know this is hard, Katie, but I need your help." Her voice was gentle, and she didn't sound upset. I think she understood. I went over to the bookcase and ran my hand along the backs of the books. I picked a few of them up and put them in the box. Without them all over the place, my room wouldn't look like it belonged to me anymore. It wouldn't be mine.

"Does it have to be packed up today?" If it didn't have to be done right away, I wanted to leave.

"I'm afraid that we have to get a start on getting things packed up. Because of the distance, we won't be able to work on it a little at a time, but will have to get as much done as we can while we have the chance." She moved on to packing what I left in the dresser, and never once stopped working. "It'll be easier to get as much as we can done now."

Easier for them maybe, but not for me. I put a few more books in the box. I couldn't stand to help take apart my own life bit by bit and put it in a box. I needed to get out. Sarah looked up in surprise as I strode over to the door and slammed it behind me.

Once outside I ran. My feet seemed to fly along, without any thought as to where I was going. They just took me. I automatically ran to my place by the river bank. Slowing to a walk, I looked out across the river.

Daddy and I went fishing a lot in the river. It was one of our favorite things to do together. When I came to my favorite tree, I looked up. The plank across the branches was still there, hidden from view. Glancing around, I climbed into the tree. I sat down on the platform and peered between the leaves. The river shimmered in the sunlight. I wanted to stay in the tree forever. No one would find me, and I wouldn't have to go back to Uncle Charley's house. They were nice to me, but I didn't belong. The heat of the day made me drowsy. I leaned up against the trunk of the tree and I fell asleep.

I jerked awake. Someone was climbing up the trunk of the tree. How could anyone find me? No one but Timmy knew about my secret place, and he would never tell.

I stood; ready to climb higher if I had to, when I saw the top of Timmy's head. "What're you doing here?"

"I could ask you the same thing." He hauled himself the rest of the way up. "I heard that your family was looking for you." Dressed in a pair of ragged jeans again, I ought to have known a suit wouldn't last long on him. "I knew you'd be here." He stared down at the boards. Timmy looked skinny, and he was shorter than Tom. I was just so glad to see such a good friend. Tim sat there, silently.

"Timmy?"

"What?" He didn't even glance up at me.

"What did you think about the funeral?" I couldn't call it my Daddy's yet.

"I don't know. What did you think?" He was hedging, and he still wouldn't look at me.

"Don't do that to me."

"Do what?"

My anger started to grow. "Everyone I know is treating me differently, acting like I might break or something." I paused for a breath. "I need something to be the same."

He finally turned his head to look at me. "I just don't know what to say. I don't want to upset you."

I looked to the top of the tree. "I'd rather be upset than to have you different too." I sat down beside him.

"You said it yourself, things have changed, and I don't know how to act."

"You never worried about how to act around me before. Timmy, you're my best friend. I don't want that to change."

His finger traced the grain on the plank. "I couldn't believe it when you left." His voice was quiet. "One minute we were together doing things like burning down sheds, and then next you were gone." I almost couldn't hear him. "I thought your Dad was joking when he told me you were gone. I knew you'd never stand to be sent away like that."

I put my hand on his arm. "I didn't want to go. You know that. I had no choice." I suddenly realized how much had changed for Timmy as well. I was his only friend and he was always welcome at our house, and not many other places. I could always tell Timmy anything.

I looked out to the river. "You know what bothers me the most? The last thing we did was argue, and I never told him how much I would miss him."

The silence grew for a moment before Timmy spoke. "You didn't have to tell him. He knew."

I stood and walked over to the edge. "I know. I just wish I had said it, that's all. I wouldn't even look at him when the bus pulled out." I hit a branch. "I wish I could do it all over again."

"You can't go back. You'll just have to go forward." He stopped for a moment. "I know. It's easy to say." He ruffled up his hair. "What'll happen now?"

I turned toward him. "I'll live with my Uncle Charley and go to school. It's the way Daddy set things up." The sky turned pink and darkened. "As much as I wanted to get out of this place and experience life, this is not what I wanted."

Timmy looked at the darkening sky. "I suppose that you have to go. They'll really be looking for you now."

"Let them."

He peered up at me. "Katie, you have to go back with them."

I walked over and sat down in front of him. "I know that. I just don't want to have to go back to the house." I swallowed to keep my voice from rising. "I don't want to go back in and see everything gone. I want to remember it the way it was." I started picking at my skirt. "That's not too much to ask, is it?"

"No." His voice was soothing. I would really miss him. "We have to leave sometime though."

"I know. Give me five minutes." We sat in silence while I got ready to go back to the house. I couldn't even call it home anymore. Darkness had fallen by the time I got up to leave.

Timmy walked me back to the house. The silence was nice,

comforting. He gave me a hug, and said good-bye. "You better write and tell me what kind of mischief you get yourself into." He gave me a little punch on the shoulder. "The one thing I'm sure of in life is that wherever you are, you're probably creating trouble of some kind."

As he left, I turned my back to the road so I didn't have to see him disappear. I always thought we'd be together. He was the closest thing to a brother I had. I felt like everything had been stripped from me in one blow. I lost my Daddy, my home, and my best friend.

They weren't finished with the packing yet, but I wouldn't go back in the house. It hurt too much. So, I opened the door of the truck and sat down to wait.

After what seemed like forever, Mark came out to talk to me. "Have you been here long?"

I had been sitting so long; my legs had gone to sleep. "A little while."

He stuck his hands in his pockets. "Looks like you need a jacket." The air had cooled off, and the goose pimples covered my arms.

I shrugged one shoulder. "I'm all right."

"We'll be leaving pretty soon, they're just about finished."

Terrific. My whole life packed up and ready to go. The back of the truck was already filled. I didn't look to see what was in it. I didn't want to know.

"I'm going to go inside and help finish up. Do you want to come?"

"No. I can't."

He nodded. "We'll all be out in a few minutes."

When he went in the front door, I could see the passageway and how empty it looked beyond. It was just a glimpse before the door closed, but it was enough. I closed my eyes, leaned my head all the way back, and took a deep breath.

A few minutes later, the door opened, and Sarah tossed my jacket on top of me. "You should put it on. It's a long trip back." I put it on and closed the door. Sarah got in and started the truck. "Uncle Charley said that we should go home now so it won't be too late when we get back."

I scrunched up in the seat to prepare for the long trip home. As I sat looking into the darkness, anger started to grow inside me. I couldn't explain it, but I felt angrier and angrier with each passing mile. I was angry at God for taking my Daddy away from me. How could he do that when I still needed him so much? I was angry at myself for not seeing that Daddy was sick earlier and making him get help in time to make him better. I was angry with Uncle Charley, he knew that my Daddy was dying when I arrived, and that's the only reason he took me. Even though it wasn't rational, I was angry at Daddy for leaving me with a family who didn't want me. I had been forced on them and they took me out of pity. Well, I didn't want or need them either.

A charity case. A stupid charity case was all I was to them. I hoped they felt righteous and holy about it. It was the sort of thing McCabes did. Taking in the homeless and unwanted made them look and feel good. It would be a bad reflection on the McCabe family name if they didn't take me in. I never felt like a member of the McCabe family, and now I felt even less like one. I felt like pushing them into breaking the McCabe tradition. They could forget about me obeying any rules they set up. I didn't want to live with them and I would let them know it.

We drove most of the way home through the night without talking. Sarah broke the silence first. "School starts tomorrow." She paused to brush a strand of hair out of the way. "Uncle Charley wants to know whether you want to go, or wait a couple of days."

I could wait a whole year. School just wasn't important anymore. "I don't know." I stared out the window into the darkness.

"Well, it's your decision." She left the end hanging like she had more to say.

I looked at her. "But you have your own opinion."

She gave a slight nod. "You have had so many changes over the past few days, it's a lot to take in, and so I understand if you need some time to adjust or if it's just too much." She paused. "You might feel like you need something to take your mind off all of the changes, something to keep you from brooding."

I doubted it. I'd just feel bad around a bunch of strangers. I stared out the window again. "All right. I'll go."

"You don't have to, if you don't want to."

Right. After she gets through telling me how school will keep me from feeling so bad, all of a sudden I don't have to go. "I'll go. It doesn't make any difference to me anyway." I could cause just as much trouble at school as I could at home. Even more if I worked at it.

"You can always go, and if it is too much, you can give me a call and come home."

Home. Such a small word, that means so much. I wasn't headed toward home; I was getting further and further away with each passing mile.

School Time Troubles

Early in the morning I woke up with a headache. Dread began to fill me as I thought about going to school. I was really getting nervous about going to a school that was so much bigger than my school at home. Tom would be there. Somehow, knowing that didn't comfort me as much as I thought it would. I pulled on my jeans and a flannel shirt to go do my chores before breakfast.

It surprised me to be the first one up. Usually I had to be dragged out of bed and forced to get ready. During the night, I tossed and turned, and never quite got comfortable. It was a relief to get out of the house into the cool morning air. I took my time doing my chores because it was nice to be alone for a while.

When I got back inside, Sarah was already up and dressed. "There you are. I wondered where you had gone." I just looked at her. "I laid out one of the dresses we brought back with us for you to wear."

Here she went with the dress bit again. "I don't want to wear one."

She pressed her lips together. "It's the first day of school and I thought you'd want to look nice."

For some reason, she didn't seem to think I could look nice in anything but a dress. "I have other clothes I can wear." Hostility put an edge in my tone. "And where do you get off picking out my clothes anyway? I'm not a toy doll you can dress up."

"I don't know why you have this thing against dresses." Her hair swirled as she shook her head. "Putting on a dress makes me feel pretty. A little more feminine after working out here on the farm, I guess."

I thought Sarah could wear a trash bag and look gorgeous, so I didn't know why she needed a dress to make her feel pretty. "I always feel like I have to be on my best behavior when wearing a dress."

"Now that's the best reason I've heard to make you wear one. Excuse me while I go throw out the rest of your clothes." She winked at me and laughed. "I'm not asking you to walk a plank or sky dive from thirty thousand feet. I just want you to make a good impression on your first day at school."

"You don't think it'll make me look too prissy or like I'm full of myself?" Or even worse, I could look like Emma. That was a new bad place in my brain.

Sarah shook her head. "Of course not. Go take your shower now and get dressed."

I looked in the mirror as I entered the bathroom and immediately felt on the verge of tears. How could so much sadness hit me so unexpectedly? One minute I was grumpy, the next pretty happy as Sarah teased me, and now my heart was so full of sorrow I thought it could burst. I took a deep breath to steady myself and realized that it was my first day of school without my Daddy. Getting ready for school, I felt like I might never be happy again.

As I walked on the campus, I felt a little strange. I didn't know hardly anyone, and the school was a lot bigger than I was used to. I didn't feel quite so out of place in my dress though, because most of the other girls I saw were wearing them too. I wondered if they wore them every day. If they did, I'd hate getting dressed for school.

Sarah came with me to look over my class schedule. Mr. Conway said he would place me in classes he thought I needed according to my test results. We arrived early so I could get a locker and find all my classes before they started.

Mr. Conway looked as prim as ever. "We were quite impressed with the results of your tests, Katie." I opened my mouth to say something, but Sarah gripped my shoulder, so I closed it again. "Coming from such a small school, I didn't expect you to score as high as you did." His glasses were about to slide off the end of his nose. "Because of your abilities, I was forced to put you in some sophomore classes."

He pushed his glasses back up and straightened his tie. "I'll keep myself informed as to how you are doing. We'll be expecting fine work from you."

Fat chance. I didn't have to do any work, and I didn't want to. He'd be keeping track of me all right, but not because of my wonderful abilities. Quite the opposite in fact. I looked at the class schedule he handed me.

Seven subjects and none of them fun. He even enrolled me in a study skills class, and I didn't need to learn how to study because I always did well in classes. Sarah held out her hand to see my class assignments. I tried to guess what she thought about it by watching her face, but I failed.

She handed back the paper, and gave me the rest of my packet which had a map of the school and my locker combination in it. She didn't look very pleased, but I couldn't tell what she was upset about. "You'd better put your things in your locker and get to your first class."

I left reluctantly, but Sarah watched me until I was out the door. I heard the murmur of voices as soon as the door clicked shut, but I couldn't hear the words. The bell for the first class would be ringing any minute, and there were a lot more kids walking around. It looked like everyone was wearing their Sunday best.

I looked at my schedule again. At least I had volleyball and track for my last class. That way I'd be outside and able to watch the guys at football practice. A shadow crossed me and I looked up.

Tom stood there grinning. "I wondered how long it'd take you to figure out I was here." He couldn't have been standing there for very long. He looked handsome in a suit and tie, a lot better than Timmy. By the look on his face, I could tell he liked my dress. Maybe Sarah hadn't been too wrong in wanting me to wear it.

"Do you dress like this every day?" I tugged at his tie.

"No. It's just kind of a school tradition for everyone to dress up on the first day of school. After that it's jeans every day."

I couldn't figure out why Sarah didn't tell me that instead of arguing with me this morning. If she told me the reason behind it, I would have put on the dress without so much of a fight. Maybe she thought I knew the tradition already.

He touched the paper. "Is this your schedule?" I handed it to him and he frowned. "Why are you taking such a heavy schedule? You'll be doing so much homework that you won't have any time for me."

I shrugged. "I didn't have any choice in the matter. Mr. Conway enrolled me." None of the classes were my choice. "Don't worry about the homework though, I just won't do any."

Tom took my things and started to walk toward the lockers. "I'm sure glad he doesn't sign me up for classes. My brain would suffer from overload." He glanced at my schedule again. "We have the same class right before lunch."

"Really?"

He grinned. "Yep. Geometry. Not the most fun in the world, but we'll liven up the class." More than he probably knew. He stopped at a locker and opened it up. He put the lunch Sarah made for me in it and shut the door again. "I'll walk you to your first class."

When we got inside the building, he stopped talking and looked straight into my eyes for a minute.

"What's wrong?"

He pulled me over to a set of carrels. "I tried to call you yesterday afternoon, but no one was home. I heard some story going around that your father was sick. How is he?"

The tears felt hot in my eyes, but I didn't want to cry in front of him. "Yesterday was his funeral."

His eyes looked pained. "I'm so sorry."

"Don't be. It happened and your being sorry can't change that." How harsh I sounded. "I didn't mean it to come out that way."

"That's all right. I understand." He grabbed my hand. "Anytime you need to talk about him, I'll listen." What a neat guy. Not many guys would honestly care so soon, and others wouldn't be so understanding. And what did I do? Practically snap his head off for talking to me about it.

First hour went really fast for some reason. I had to tell who I was and something about myself. I felt like saying my name and this was the last place on the earth that I wanted to be. Mr. Whitehall then told us what to expect in his class. I sat in the back of the room and kids kept turning around to look at me. I wasn't meaning to cause a disturbance this time, it just happened naturally.

One guy in the class started to shoot paper wads at some of his friends. Mr. Whitehall kept reading from his page of rules and requirements, unaware of the wads flying through the air. The guy shot a paper wad at me, and I flicked it back. The paper wad war began. I collected five at a time and then rapid fire shot them back.

Unfortunately, or fortunately, depending on how I wanted to look at it, during one of my sessions a wad hit the teacher and he stopped reading. He bent down and picked up the wad. "Who is responsible for this?" He glared at the class, trying to stare us down. I still had three wads lined up on my desk. Seizing my chance while he was looking at another section of the class, I flicked them off my desk as fast as I could. I shot them as close to Mr. Whitehall as possible, and the last one struck him. Pay dirt.

His head swung quickly around. "This behavior must stop!" He slammed his roll book on the desk and his face turned a bright red. "If the guilty party does not confess, the entire class will be on Saturday school clean-up."

A lot of kids started groaning and looking around the room. The guy who started it just looked at the ceiling. I looked around the room for a moment, and then stood up.

"Does this mean that you are the guilty party, Miss McCabe?" What did he think? That I stood up for my health? I nodded my head. "Did you make this mess by yourself, or did you have some help?"

He was asking me to snitch on someone, and I couldn't do that. Especially on the first day of school. I'd never live it down. The whole class waited for me to say something. The guy who started the war kept throwing me dirty looks, as if I might keep quiet because of them. Mr. Whitehall stood with his arms folded across his chest glaring at me. If I wanted to create some problems, this seemed like the perfect time.

"It doesn't matter if I had any help or not. You wanted a confession? You got one." He wouldn't be satisfied with that and I knew it.

"Miss McCabe, you are showing a definite negative attitude. I asked you a simple question."

Negative attitude? What a joke. "You asked me to turn in a classmate. I won't do that. Not for something this stupid."

He walked over to his desk and opened up a drawer. "In that case, come up to the front of the room." I slowly moved to the front. He pulled out a pad of referral slips. "If you won't cooperate, I have no choice but to refer you to the Vice Principal."

I grit my teeth. "Send me. I don't cave in to threats."

He handed me the slip, and I left the class, giving a mock salute before walking out the door. Things were working out better than I expected. Uncle Charley didn't really want me. I'd show him how much trouble charity cases could be.

The receptionist gave me a friendly smile as I walked into the office. "May I help you with something?"

I held up the blue referral slip. "Mr. Whitehall sent me to see the Vice Principal."

She calmly picked up the phone and rang Mr. Segerstrom's office. "He's free to see you now."

I started to get a little nervous because I wasn't quite sure what to expect. The Vice Principal of my old school and I had been good friends, if for no other reason than I had been to see him several times during the course of the years. Well, they couldn't do anything to me that hadn't already been done. I turned the knob and walked boldly in.

Mr. Segerstrom looked different than I expected. For some reason, I thought he might look like Mr. Conway, but he was tall and had an athletic build instead. I handed him my slip.

"Well Katie, I think you'd better sit down for a moment." He folded his hands on the desk and leaned forward. "I don't know what kind of rules you were used to in your previous school, but I want you to know that throwing paper wads around the room is not acceptable here."

Did he seriously think that throwing paper wads was acceptable in any school? He paused as if he expected me to say something, but I kept silent. "Since this is your first day here, I'm going to let you go with a warning." He settled back in his chair. "I did not expect to have someone in my office quite so soon." How fun. I got to be the first discipline problem of the year. "What bothers me more than the incident itself is the note Mr. Whitehall wrote on your slip. Something about an uncooperative attitude."

I had to bite the end of my tongue to keep from laughing. I didn't know whether to tell him why Mr. Whitehall had put that down or not. Mr. Segerstrom sat quietly waiting for me to speak.

"I don't know how to put this." I paused to search for the right words. "Mr. Whitehall asked me to turn someone else in. I won't do that." I shifted uncomfortably in my chair. "I'd rather take the blame for the whole thing." I couldn't help myself from continuing. "Can you imagine what would happen if I ratted someone out in my first class of a new school? I'd be crucified. It was unfair of him to ask me to do that." A hint of a smile crossed his face. "That's the reason he sent me here. Not because of the mess I made, or anything like that. But because I wouldn't tell him who else had been involved."

Mr. Segerstrom stroked his jaw. "I'll accept that. I hope that this becomes an isolated incident, and that you will not make being sent to my office a habit." Exactly what I intended to do. "Remember that I am letting you off this time. If there is a next time, I will have to contact your guardian."

I couldn't tell him that I wished he would contact Uncle Charley. It would make things a lot easier for me if he did.

Second period already started by the time I left the office, so I took an excuse note for being tardy. I didn't look at the class when I walked in, but went straight to the teacher, Miss Phelps, and gave her my excuse. "Why don't you take that empty seat next to Emma?"

I hoped against hope that the Emma would not be the same one I met at the picnic, but it was. I searched the room quickly to see if there were any other empty seats, but they were all filled. I'd make sure that I was on time in this class tomorrow so I could get a seat away from her. As I sat down in my seat, Miss Phelps continued class. "I am sending around a seating chart. Please write your name on the chart where you are now sitting. This will be your permanent seat for the semester."

I couldn't believe what I was hearing. I would have to be stuck next to Emma for an entire semester. I hadn't done anything bad enough to deserve that. A girl sat next to me on the other side too. Not that I didn't like girls, I just seemed to get along better with guys for some reason.

I heard a hissing to the side of me. "Katie."

I turned toward Emma. "What?"

"Just don't talk to me."

Me? Talk to her? Who did she think she was trying to fool? "Don't worry. I don't want to take a chance on catching what you've got." I didn't want it to get around that I sat next to her, let alone talked to her.

"What do you mean?" Emma's voice started to rise above a whisper.

"Something must have happened to make you that ugly. I figured it must have been a disease of some kind, and I don't want to get it."

Her face started turning red with anger. "Of all the mean. . ."

A shadow fell across us and I looked up. Miss Phelps was standing in front of us with her arms folded across her chest. "Is there some sort of problem here girls?"

Emma pulled herself up straight in her chair as her face returned to its normal pasty complexion. "No, Miss Phelps. Since Katie is new here, I was trying to help her out by answering some questions she had."

Emma was such a liar and so two-faced, I couldn't believe it. "That isn't the impression I got when I walked up here. I'd like you both to come back to my room after school and we'll discuss the matter further then."

Detention. If I couldn't get Mr. Segerstrom to send a note home with me, then at least I could say that I got detention. It was a start. Not only that, but I'd managed to get Emma into trouble too. She kept shooting me dirty looks, and even went as far as to write a note telling me she'd get me back. But, she didn't open her mouth for the rest of the class time. I wished I could do that more often.

I practically slept through my third class, it was so boring. If it stayed that way, I'd have to find some way to liven it up. I hurried to my fourth class so I could sit next to Tom. I wasn't that thrilled about being in a Geometry class, but I would make it through somehow. What came as a shock was that Harvey was in the class too. I didn't think he had the brains for it, but I supposed that there might be one thing in the world that he could do. Besides being a rotten person.

The class started off slow and quiet, the same as any other class on the first day. Mrs. Johnson wanted to get the textbooks out to us right away because she wanted us to do a couple review problems. That way we could take a test sometime during this first week to see how much we had retained over the summer. Homework on the first day of school. I knew this was not going to be a class I enjoyed.

Harvey passed out the books. When he got to me, he slammed the book down on my hand. Without pausing to think I picked it up and swung it around hitting him on the arm with it. I was getting ready to swing it again when I heard Mrs. Johnson talking to me.

"Young lady. Put that book down this instant." I went ahead and followed through hitting Harvey once again before I put the book back on the desk. "That is not acceptable in this classroom." Acceptable seemed to be the buzz word for the day. She pulled out her pad of referral slips. "Take this down to Mr. Segerstrom's office, and he will handle it from here."

A second trip to the Vice Principal in one day. What an accomplishment. Harvey smirked at me as I walked out the door. I wondered what Tom thought about the whole situation. He was probably angry with Harvey for getting me into trouble. Well, Harvey would just have to look out for himself.

The receptionist didn't give the same friendly smile when I walked through the door this time. She didn't even ask what I needed, just motioned me to go on into Mr. Segerstrom's office. Mrs. Johnson must have called ahead and warned her of my coming.

"Take a seat Katie." Mr. Segerstrom frowned as I came through the door. "I don't think I have to tell you how upset I am to have you back here in my office today." He held out his hand. "I need your blue slip." He glanced at it, but it looked like he already knew what it said. "Do you have any excuse or justification for this sort of action?"

What was I supposed to say to something like that? "The guy handing out the books slammed mine down on my hand. On purpose." I shrugged. "I lost my temper."

He leaned forward to glare at me better. "That does not justify what you did."

That made me mad. "I never said it did. Did you want to know what happened, or not?"

He took out a sheet of paper. "All right. Now, I am going to write a note to your Uncle, and you will have to bring it back to me signed by him before going to any classes tomorrow."

I wondered what he was writing down. He paused once or twice while writing, then signed it, and sealed it in an envelope. "Since you ended up here twice in one day, I informed your Uncle of both incidents." Uncle Charley'd be wondering what he'd got himself into. "I don't want to see you for the rest of the day, unless it's passing by between classes."

I stood up and took the letter.

"Tell my receptionist that you will be coming in to see me tomorrow morning before your first class, and you are to come right in.

By the time I got back to class, it was almost over. Mrs. Johnson had assigned forty problems of various types for us to do for the next class. If she was going to assign homework like that for the whole semester, it was going to be a very long one. Either that or I'd voluntarily flunk it. That might not be a bad idea anyway. I'd just plan on not doing my homework for tomorrow for starters. The last few minutes of class drug by at a snail's pace. I wanted it to be over so we could go to lunch, and I could talk to Tom.

"Class dismissed." I thought I'd never hear those words, possibly some of the best words in the English language. I grabbed my book and I was ready to go.

Tom took my hand as we stepped out the door. "So did Mr. Segerstrom go light with you because it was your first time? He usually does."

I slowly shook my head. "It was my second time."

"What do you mean?" Tom stopped for a minute and looked at me.

"I got sent in first hour too."

He sat down on one of the benches. "How come?"

"For doing stupid stuff. I don't want to talk about it." I'd have enough time to do that tonight. "It doesn't matter anyway. I just have to take a note home and have it signed."

"Won't you get into trouble?" Tom looked concerned.

"Probably." Definitely would have been a more accurate response.

"Why doesn't it matter?"

"Because they don't care about me." They'd just be mad because I caused problems, not because I meant anything to them. "I might get into trouble, but I don't care. What can they do to me anyway?" We sat for the rest of the lunch time not saying much. A troubled expression kept crossing Tom's face. "Don't worry about it. I'll be fine."

"I just want you to know that I like you, and want to know what happens to you." His hand slipped over mine. "Call me tonight and let me know what your Uncle said. If you can't call for some reason, come to school a little early tomorrow so I have a chance to see you." Lunch was over and I didn't want to leave. That seemed to happen every time I was around Tom.

The rest of the day went by quickly. Emma and I got lectured to by Miss Phelps for about half an hour after school, and told us that she expected no further problems. She expected us to learn tolerance of each other. All I'd learn was how much of a pain Emma was, and I knew that to begin with.

Sarah was waiting in the parking lot for me when I came out. "You're a little late, aren't you?"

I wasn't even in the truck yet and she started quizzing me. "I had to stay after for one of my classes."

She threw me a sharp look. "Is this something we need to discuss at home?"

"I don't care if we talk about it now or later."

She swatted my leg. "You watch your tone of voice."

We pulled up in the drive a couple of minutes later. I didn't wait for the truck to come to a complete stop before I jumped out and ran into the house. I went straight into my room.

Sarah came in as soon as she parked the truck. "I want to know what happened at school."

I looked at the floor. "Emma and I got into an argument in my second class, so the teacher gave us detention." I flopped down on the bed. "It was no big deal."

Sarah pressed her lips angrily together. "Since it was no big deal, you can stay in your room until Uncle Charley gets home. Then you can talk to him about it."

And a few other things. "Won't you need my help in the kitchen?" I tried to be as sarcastic as possible.

"Not tonight I won't." She left the room.

I laughed. A couple hours to myself were a blessing. I could take a nap. Maybe I was supposed to be thinking about what I had done wrong. Perhaps feel a little sorry about it. I just lay down and went to sleep.

I woke up to someone roughly shaking my shoulder. Sarah. "It's time to eat."

I came out and sat at the table. As soon as grace was said, the inquisition started. Uncle Charley picked up his fork and glanced over at me. "Sarah tells me you had a problem at school today. I'd like to discuss it."

I wasn't going to bring up the trips to the Vice Principal's office until after dinner, but I decided I might as well throw it at them all at once. "Which problem?"

Sarah turned to look at me. "You only mentioned one problem."

"So? I had a couple others. You only asked me about one."

Her eyes narrowed. "I asked you what happened at school."

Uncle Charley cleared his throat. "Katie, you need to tell us what went on today at school. All of it."

I jumped up from the table and went into my room to get the note from Mr. Segerstrom. "I'm supposed to give this to you. I guess now is as good a time as any."

I ate hurriedly while Uncle Charley read the note, his face growing grimmer as he went down the page. He came to the end and put the letter on the table. "You are excused from the table to go to your room." I started to open my mouth to protest, but Uncle Charley held up his hand. "No arguments. Go."

I never got to eat a meal around this place. I knew that it wouldn't be long before he came in to talk to me, so I sat on the edge of my bed and waited.

When Uncle Charley came in he was quiet and calm. I expected him to still be angry. "I brought home a bicycle for you to use to get to and from school."

How unexpected. I thought he'd yell at me, not give me a bicycle. "Thanks." I knew I didn't sound very grateful, but I had been thrown off balance.

He walked over and sat on Sarah's bed. "Did you get all your classes squared away?"

I didn't understand his beating around the bush. It put me on edge. "I suppose so. Mr. Conway made up my class schedule." I ran my hand through my hair. "He gave me a pretty heavy load."

"I'm sure you'll be able to handle it." He looked straight into my eyes. "Do you have anything to say for yourself?" He looked hurt.

"I guess not." He continued to just look at me. "What do you want from me?" I didn't like being stared at like that, especially since he wasn't saying anything more. "It's just something that happened. I suppose I could have helped it if I had wanted to." I looked down at my hands. How much more could I say? I wasn't going to apologize.

"I want you to clean up the kitchen tonight, and tomorrow when you get home from school, Sarah will have a list of extra chores for you to do." He stood up. "After you are through with the kitchen, you are to do any homework that you have and get into bed."

It was the same routine as usual, work and then bed. I cleaned the kitchen in silence. When I was through, I picked up the phone to call Tom.

Sarah stared at me. "What do you think you are doing?"

"I'm making a phone call. What does it look like?" I held the receiver in my hand. What else could I be doing?

"Put down the phone." Her voice had that hard edge to it again.

"All I'm going to do is call someone. Don't get so upset." I didn't understand what the problem was.

Sarah stormed over to the phone, took the receiver from my hand and hung it up. "You are not making any phone calls tonight."

Who did she think she was anyway? "It sure didn't take you long to start ordering me around." She glared at me.

"Katie, it's time you went to your room." Now Uncle Charley was picking on me. At least he had the right to.

I ran into the room and slammed the door as hard as I could. On the edge of tears again, I grabbed my teddy bear and flopped down on the bed. I think what bothered me the most was that I got into trouble in front of Matt and Mark. If they had jumped on me too, it would have been too much for me. Especially Matt.

I avoided looking at Matt when Uncle Charley was reading the letter from Mr. Segerstrom. It would have reminded me of Daddy and I didn't need that right now. I needed to forget my Daddy and what he would have thought or felt about things. If I could forget him, maybe I wouldn't hurt so much inside. If I could forget him, it would make it easier to hate these people, and easier for me not to care about hurting them.

The next day flew by. I started meeting a lot of people at school, and making new friends. Tom really helped out in that area because he knew almost everyone on campus, and he introduced me to everyone he met. Plus, with the number of times I had already been in trouble of one kind or another, my reputation for being a rebel was spreading. I saw Mike between classes and Pete and I sat next to one another in English.

Wednesday morning dawned bright, and I actually felt good about going to school. The bicycle that Uncle Charley bought me rode like a dream, and it only took about fifteen minutes to get to school. The morning air was crisp, and began to feel like fall. Sarah had the radio on while we were getting ready, and the weather forecaster predicted a rainstorm within the next two days, but looking at the sky I could hardly believe it. Storms belonged to another age, not this one.

I hurried through my morning tasks so I could get to school a little early to spend some time with Tom. We decided to spend a few minutes together each morning, with no one else around so we could talk. He was such a neat guy; he really seemed to understand what I was going through and wanted to help me through it. We disagreed about whether Uncle Charley and the rest of the family really wanted me to live with them or not, but we respected each other's opinions.

As I parked my bike, I thought I saw Harvey near my locker, but when I looked again, he was gone. I must have been imagining things. Why imagine something as awful as Harvey on such a good morning, I'd never know.

"Did things go better for you yesterday?" I jumped. Tom liked to come out of nowhere and start talking to me.

"A little." Of course, I hadn't been in any trouble at school either. I'd see what I could do about fixing that today.

"Are you ready for our Geometry test today?"

I made a face. "I think it's ridiculous to have a test the third day of class. What does she expect us to know at this point?" I leaned against the wall. "I wouldn't mind so much if she wasn't using it as a part of our grade. What happens if we really bomb this test?"

Tom shrugged his shoulders. "I don't know what to tell you. You should do fine on it."

I paused for a moment. "What if I don't want to?"

Tom turned away. "Katie, don't do this."

Here we went again. "Why shouldn't I? If you feel so strong about it, tell me."

He paused. "You'll only be hurting yourself anyway."

"How can you say that? I just don't care anymore, so they can't hurt me." I knew they would get riled because school was important to the McCabe clan.

"You may upset them for awhile, but you're the one who has to live with the grades." Tom licked and bit his lower lip. "And try to get into a decent college with them."

I hadn't thought that far ahead. "Freshman year grades don't go on the college transcripts though, do they?" He shook his head. I raised my shoulders. "Well then?"

"You still have to get into the college prep classes based on how you do this year."

I wrinkled my nose. He was right; I couldn't afford not to do well. "All right. I'll do my best on this one."

He gave a huge sigh of relief. "I wasn't sure you were going to listen to reason. You'll be glad you did in the long run." The bell for class rang so we had to leave one another again.

Walking into second period, I shuddered. I dreaded coming to the class because of Emma. She either completely ignored me, or wrote me nasty notes. I preferred being ignored. I sat down and Emma turned toward me. It didn't look like she was going to ignore me today.

"Hello Katie, how are you today?" Emma smiled at me.

I couldn't believe it. The goody two shoes had returned. "Just fine, thanks." It took all I had to be civil to her.

"Good. Harvey told me you're having a test in Geometry. Are you ready for it?"

I couldn't figure out why she turned on her fake charm. "I think so." I wondered what she was up to, or what she wanted from me. She made me ill with her false sincerity.

"Good luck on it."

Class started and Emma had to stop talking to me. She was probably as relieved as I was. The morning passed quickly and Geometry class came sooner than I expected. The test went well. I didn't have any problems with it at all. I finished the test first, so I waited in the hall until Tom came out.

"So? How'd you do?" He grabbed my books.

"I think I got them all right. How'd you do?"

He grinned. "I did pretty well. I may have missed one or two, but no more than that."

We spent the whole lunch hour talking and joking around. Mike joined us about half way through, and he teased me the rest of the time. It was the most relaxing time I'd spent since coming to this place. I couldn't explain why I felt so comfortable with Tom, but I always felt like I could just be me and he would accept me as I was. The only person in my life, other than my Daddy, that made me feel that way was Timmy and I had known him all my life.

Walking into study skills, the room seemed dingier than usual. After having been out in the bright sunlight, it took a couple minutes to adjust to the light inside. Class started with its usual dreariness, I was getting tired of lecture after lecture of what the study environment should be and what the different learning styles were and wished we could get on to something a little more exciting. Of course, the next topic promised to be just as boring; the five methods of note-taking. We had only been at it for about five minutes when one of the office workers came in with a message for the teacher.

"Katie." She walked over to my desk. "Mr. Segerstrom would like to see you in his office."

I wondered what he wanted me for. I hadn't done anything wrong that I could think of. I picked up my things and left class. The secretary waved me right into his office when I walked through the door. It was beginning to feel like a familiar habit.

False Accusations and Vandalism

"Have a seat, Katie." Mr. Segerstrom did not look happy. "I've called you in to discuss a serious matter." I didn't figure he'd called me in to talk about the weather. "Some students have accused you of stealing a copy of the master of the Geometry test you took today." I felt a jolt in the pit of my stomach. "With the accusation, I had Mrs. Johnson grade your paper right away and you scored one hundred percent. She feels that your score is suspicious as you have been struggling with the homework." I hadn't been struggling; I had deliberately not done some of the homework. This was the one time when missing a few answers on a test would have been a good thing. "I wanted to give you the chance to defend yourself."

I couldn't believe it. Stealing a test master never even occurred to me. "I didn't do it, if that's what you're asking me."

He gave a brief smile. "Yes, that was what I was asking. I'm going to ask you to allow me to look in your locker." What did he want to look in my locker for? I told him I didn't do it. "The students who made the accusation said they saw you put the master in your locker this morning."

That answered that question. "Sure." I shrugged. "Why should I mind? There's nothing there that shouldn't be." I stood up.

"Nothing would make me happier than to find exactly that."

As we walked to my locker, I felt very self-conscious about having the Vice Principal follow me the entire way. Fortunately, classes were still in session. It would have been embarrassing to have to do this while everyone passed between classes. The curiosity of my new friends would have been too much for me. In a way, I did mind that he had asked me to see the inside of my locker, but I understood why he had to look.

We walked without talking, and when we arrived at the locker, the only sound was the scraping of the lock as I turned it. I swung the door open. "There you go."

He systematically took everything out of my locker, looking at each piece of paper, and shaking out the books. Nothing. Even though I knew I hadn't done it, I breathed a sigh of relief. He pulled out the last book, and there was a piece of paper I didn't remember seeing before. It was probably one of my math papers that had slipped out of the book and slid down the side.

He looked at it. "If you didn't steal the master, how do you explain this?"

I looked in total disbelief at what he held in his hand. It was a copy of the Geometry test. "I don't know. I didn't take it." It sounded lame, even to my ears.

"Let's go back to my office." I could tell by the tone of his voice I wouldn't be able to talk my way out of this one.

Besides, I didn't know what to say or do. It was hard to argue that I hadn't done something when he held the 'proof' in his hand that I had. I didn't know what he would do with me. My stomach started twisting into knots.

We got back to his office and he still didn't say anything more to me. He placed the master on his desk, and pulled out a sheet of blank paper. Maybe he was writing Uncle Charley again. The silence made me nervous, and the scratching of the pen on the paper nearly drove me up a wall. He signed his name to the paper and put his pen down. Then he reached for the phone. "I'd like to speak with Mr. McCabe, please."

The note hadn't been to Uncle Charley then. I wondered who he had written to. "Mr. McCabe, this is Ed Segerstrom. I have your niece here in my office right now."

I couldn't believe he was calling with me in the room. Maybe he wanted me to hear exactly what he said to Uncle Charley. "She was accused of stealing a test, which she denied, but I found a copy of the test in her locker." Somebody had planted it there, but I couldn't prove anything. "I'm sending her home now; she's been suspended for the rest of the day." Suspended. I had never been suspended before. "And I have placed her on Saturday clean-up for a month." That would be a barrel of laughs. "Plus, she will receive a zero for her test score."

I wouldn't have failed it that badly if I had tried to. Never having cheated on any test in my life, I couldn't believe this was happening to me. Mr. Segerstrom finished the conversation, and hung up the phone. "I wanted you to hear what I told your Uncle so you would have no doubts or question as to what he had been told." He picked up the letter he had written and folded it into thirds. "This is to Mrs. Johnson so she can re-grade your paper accordingly."

I thought about protesting my innocence once again, but I knew that it wouldn't help. He thought I was guilty, and it didn't matter at all whether I was or not. I couldn't really blame him. If I didn't know for sure that I hadn't done it, I'd have thought I was guilty too.

He let me go after telling me the regulations of Saturday clean-up. I had to leave the campus because of my suspension, but I didn't want to go home. Sarah would be there, and if Uncle Charley hadn't called her already, I'd have to explain why I was home early. It was not going to be a fun afternoon. On the way home, I tried to think of a way that the master could have been placed in my locker.

There were only two people who hated me enough to have done it. Harvey and Emma. I didn't know anyone else well enough for them to have a grudge against me. The other people I had met were friendly, and I really didn't think they would do something like this to someone they barely knew. If Emma had something to do with it, that would explain her odd behavior in class. I just wished there were a way for me to prove it.

Then I remembered seeing Harvey near my locker before school. I had actually seen him. It wasn't imagination after all. Of course, I couldn't prove that he had been there, or even what he had done. It was comforting to know that he had done it though, and I'd find a way to get him back for it. It couldn't be anything as simple as dumping him in the lake this time. That would be too good for him.

I wheeled my bike up the drive half hoping that Sarah wouldn't be home. No such luck. I parked the bike by the barn, took a deep breath, and then went in the house. Sarah looked up from the book she was studying. "Hi, Katie." She glanced at the clock on the wall. "What are you doing home so early?"

Uncle Charley must not have called. "I got sent home from school." I steeled myself for the reaction.

She closed her text book. "What for?"

How could I explain it without it seeming like I was guilty? "Mr. Segerstrom thinks that I stole the master copy to my Geometry test."

Sarah's mouth dropped open. "How could you do such a thing?" She thought I had done it too.

"I didn't." I hated having to stick up for my innocence.

"But I thought you said. . ."

I cut her off. "I didn't say I had done it. I said that Mr. Segerstrom thinks I did." I couldn't keep the irritability out of my voice. I was tired of being falsely accused.

"What would give him an idea like that?" She pursed her lips. "Why did he send you home?"

"Because he thinks I did steal the test. He found a copy of it in my locker." My anger was at the boiling point.

"There's no need to yell at me. I'm just asking some questions."

Yeah. Question after question. "It sounds like you don't believe me." There. Let her answer that one.

"I'm trying, Katie. It's just hard for me to believe something without the whole story." I couldn't convince her on the evidence either because I didn't know the whole story. "Do you know how the copy came to be in your locker?"

If I knew how to prove it, I wouldn't be standing here right now. "How am I supposed to know? Someone else must have put it there."

If I told her that Harvey put it there, she'd think I was making the whole thing up for sure. I wished my denials didn't sound so phony. If I had done it, I would have had better excuses.

"You said you didn't do it, and I'm trying to find something to help me believe that." She obviously didn't believe me though.

"What happened to the accused being innocent until proven guilty?" She didn't have anything to say to that. "I didn't really expect the Vice Principal to believe me, but I hoped that you would." I tried to glare at Sarah, but she wouldn't look at me. She turned and picked up the phone. "What're you doing?"

Sarah paused and took a deep breath. "Regardless of what you think I believe Uncle Charley has to be called." She started to push the buttons on the phone.

"But you don't have to do that. Mr. Segerstrom already called Uncle Charley when he had me in his office."

She put the receiver back down. "Katie, you assume that I don't believe you, but I'm trying to keep an open mind." She would keep it open to the fact that I had stolen the test. "I just don't know what to think. You tell me you didn't steal the test, but Mr. Segerstrom obviously thinks you did."

I grit my teeth. "I wish my Daddy were still alive. He'd tell you I didn't do it. He'd believe me."

"I'd like to believe you, but the test was found in your locker."

I knew she would think that pointed to my guilt. "I didn't put it there. Do you honestly think if I did steal the test, I'd be stupid enough to keep the copy in my locker?"

She pressed her lips together. "I think you should settle down." Tired of being told to settle down, I turned and stomped out of the room. I don't know how they expected me to stay calm when I had been accused of something I didn't do. "I didn't say we were through discussing it." Sarah followed me into the hall.

"You're not listening to me." I started yelling again. "I'm not perfect, but I don't steal, I don't cheat, and I don't lie." She put her hand on my shoulder and propelled me toward our bedroom. I shook her hand off. "It's just not fair. You're taking Mr. Segerstrom's side."

She walked back over to the door. "You may stay in here until you calm down and can talk rationally about this."

I'd be in here forever. I sat down on the edge of the bed and angrily crossed my arms. I felt like throwing something. Maybe I should decide what to do to Harvey instead of using my energy to be angry. I wanted to get him somehow. If I could get my hands on him, I'd whip the tar out of him. That at least would give me some satisfaction.

Of course, if I beat him up, I'd be in trouble again and that wouldn't be fair to me. I really didn't mind getting into trouble for things that I had done, but this time, I hadn't done anything to deserve the punishment I was sure I would get. I already had a bad mark on my school record from it, and I would have to spend a boring month cleaning up the school by picking up trash. And of course, I failed the test I promised Tom I would do well on. That I had done well on. I deserved the perfect score.

I flopped back on the bed and tried to think of different things I could do to Harvey. I'd include Emma in whatever revenge I came up with. Because of her sickening niceness to me, she had to know what was going on at least, if she hadn't helped steal the master in the first place. I could always sabotage his locker. I'd have to break into it by picking the lock somehow. Of course, I could just break the locker itself, and then he'd have to get a new one. That would ruin the purpose of booby-trapping it though because he'd know that something was wrong.

I'd have to think it out a little bit. He rode his bike to school too, and I could go over to his house and do something to his tires. Maybe fix it so they would come off while he was riding it. They both sounded like such good ideas, that I couldn't decide which one I wanted to do. As I thought about it, my eyelids got heavier and heavier, and without realizing it, I drifted off to sleep.

"Katie. It's time for supper."

Startled, I woke up. Sarah stood waiting for me. I groggily got up and went out to the table. Matt and Mark must have been told about what happened at school because neither one of them looked at me when I came into the room. I sat down at the table and still felt half asleep.

Uncle Charley started in on me as soon as grace was said. "Katie, I think you and I have something to talk about."

I didn't even have a chance to start eating. "Can't it wait until we're through? I'm not all the way awake yet."

Uncle Charley tapped his fork on the side of his dish. "I suppose we can wait until after supper."

What a relief. I didn't feel like arguing about the matter at all, let alone while we were eating. The meal was over quickly, and no one said much during it. After I finished clearing the table and washing the dishes, I went into the family room and sat down.

"Tell me what happened at school today."

Here we went again. I'd explain and they wouldn't believe me. "I was called into Mr. Segerstrom's office during fifth period, and he told me that some students said I stole a copy of the master for the Geometry test I had taken earlier." So far, so good. "I denied doing that, so Mr. Segerstrom asked if he could look through my locker." Uncle Charley sat quietly listening to my every word. "I told him no problem and he went with me to check through it. He found a copy of the master, but I had no idea how it got there." Matt looked stricken. I wished he would leave the room. "That's basically it. I didn't do it."

Uncle Charley silently tapped his finger against his cheek. "Katie, I don't know what to tell you." But he'd think of something. "You are telling me one thing, but the evidence, by your own words, says another." He was going to believe the evidence. "I'm going to have to ask you to come straight home from school for the next few weeks." Mark stood up and paced back and forth. "Also, you won't be able to attend any social activities at school, or in town." Generally, I was grounded until further notice.

"Don't you think you're being a little hard on her?" Mark was the angry one now. He seemed to take my side. "She says she didn't do it. I think you should take her word for it." At last, someone who believed me.

"I'd like to Mark, but I have to uphold my position as her guardian."

"That stinks." He angrily sat down.

"Mark, he's wrong, and so is Mr. Segerstrom, but I can't prove anything." Not yet anyway. "It would be nice if everyone else trusted me like you." It amazed me how calm I was. I think I could be because I was planning revenge. I got up. "If that's all, I have some homework to do."

Uncle Charley nodded, so I left the room. I had no intentions of doing any homework. I figured they might leave me alone for a little while if I said I had some though.

I went into the bathroom to borrow a couple things from Matt and Mark. When I walked into the bedroom, I made sure the door was shut tight. I went straight across the room. I had to be able to get the screen off the window and out of it before Sarah came in, and I had to do it quietly. My hands fumbled with the latch, and I slid the window up as slowly as I could. Every time it squeaked, I stopped to listen. Sweat started pouring down my forehead. Finally, the window was open far enough. I popped the screen out onto the ground.

I grabbed my sweatshirt jacket and the things from the bathroom, and crawled out the window. All I needed was about five minutes to get away. If I had that much time before anyone walked into the room, they wouldn't know where I had gone. I didn't bother to take the time to close the window or put the screen back on. They would know just by walking into the room that I was not there, whether the window was open or not. Besides, if I made it back before anyone knew I was gone, I'd have to use the window to get back in again.

I ran to the barn to get my bike, and a few necessary tools. I carried my jacket, still too hot to put it on. The barn door creaked loudly as I tried to open it. I paused again to listen for signs of someone coming. I took a slow, deep breath before continuing.

The moon shone brightly down, and I wished a cloud would cross over it and cover it up. I could think of other nights I'd like to spend with a bright moon, but this was not one of them. I'd have to be more careful about being seen because of the light. At least the clothes I had on were dark. Blue jeans, and when I put on my navy jacket, it would cover up my lighter colored shirt.

I stepped into the barn and waited for my eyes to adjust to the darkness. I couldn't turn on the light for fear of it being seen from the house. I wanted to move quickly, but I didn't want to make any sound.

The animals were getting restless, and they started making noise. Quickening my step, I tripped over a stool, and landed on the ground with a thud.

I lay there for a moment trying to breathe. The wind had been knocked out of me, and I was shaken completely through. After getting my breath back, I picked myself up from the ground and tried to dust myself off. I couldn't seem to stay clean around this place.

I finally made it to the tool chest, and pulled out a wrench and a screwdriver. I shoved them into my back pocket, and then grabbed a hammer, just in case. I managed to get out of the barn without running into anything else and swung the door shut. My hands kept slipping off the clasp from a combination of dirt and sweat. I wiped my hands off on my pants, and then was able to latch the door.

Unlocking my bicycle, I wheeled it past the house before getting on and riding it. I thought it would be best to go by the school first and fix the lockers, then go on to the houses. Once away from the house I started to breathe a little easier. Even if they did notice I was gone now, they'd have to search to find me.

Along the main road, I rode close to the edge, trying to keep in the shadows. I heard the sound of a car coming from behind me. I jumped off the bike and laid it down as quickly as possible. I crouched down in the brush and waited for it to pass.

The headlights loomed from around the corner and seemed to penetrate the bushes. I hoped the lights would not hit the metal on the bike and make it shine. The car sped past, and I saw that it wasn't any of the family. I felt a little dumb because I panicked so easily. I hoped no one else came along the road while I was on it.

When I came to the turn-off for the school, I wanted to make sure that no one saw me entering the school grounds. That way no one could give evidence against me. I took care to hide my bike well in some bushes alongside the school.

It took less time than I thought to break into Harvey's locker. It was a mess. I stacked his books and wound some string around them. I filled a cup with water, poked a hole through the top and tied the string to it, then to the lock itself. For the final touch, I sprayed shaving cream all over everything, making it nice and messy, and then shut the door.

It took me longer to make the mess than it did to pick the lock. Next I did Emma's locker in the same way I had done Harvey's. The only difference was that her locker was neater to start with. Despite her cleanliness, I did find an interesting note from Harvey asking if she was able to get the test master.

I couldn't believe what fools they were, leaving a note like that just lying around. If Harvey kept anything like that, I would have never known it because his locker was too much of a disaster area. I pocketed the note. I could use it later to make them pay for the false accusations I had gone through.

Finished at the school, I rode over to Emma's house. I parked my bike around the corner from her house and walked up to it as quietly as I could. I didn't know if she kept hers on the side of the house, or in the backyard. If it were in the house, I wouldn't have a chance to fix it up for her. I had no luck in finding the bike in either place.

I stood outside the house, frustrated, not knowing quite what to do. I re-climbed the fence into the backyard, and paced by the side of the house. There was a door leading into the garage with a window. I walked over and peered in. Success at last.

I cautiously tried the door handle. It opened without a fight. It only took about fifteen minutes to dismantle the front tire and make it look like it was still attached. One more stop, and then I would have to get home as fast as I could. The extra time I spent on Harvey's locker and finding Emma's bike really hurt my schedule.

Harvey's house was toward the outskirts of town, in the opposite direction from where I lived. I quickly found Harvey's bicycle next to the trash cans around the side of the house. I knelt down beside it and put my tools to work once again. The dogs in the neighborhood kept barking, and I stopped every so often to listen for anything strange going on.

It almost felt like someone was watching me. I finished with the tire, and decided I would fix Harvey's chain also. With a little luck, he'd get a couple blocks away, and the chain would fall off. After he put that back on and continued riding, the tire should come off a couple of blocks later.

I just got the chain into its place when I heard a footstep behind me. I turned quickly around. The beam of a strong flashlight hit me squarely in the eyes.

All I could see were two shiny, black shoes with legs sticking out of them. I looked further up. I kept trying to see who it was, but because of the light in my eyes, I couldn't.

"Who is that?" I put my hand in front of my eyes to shield them from the glare. "Do you want the light to blind me or something?" I closed my eyes and stood up. Maybe the light wouldn't be as bad then.

"Can I ask you what you're doing here?" The man's voice was deep, and not one that I recognized.

He moved the flashlight as I got up, so the beam still blinded me. "Why should I tell you that? I don't even know who you are." Not knowing who it was scared me a little, but I was determined to bluff my way through.

"I don't suggest you take that tone with me." He slowly lowered the flashlight.

It was a policeman, and here I was mouthing off to him. "I'm sorry Officer." I took a closer look. My heart sank.

"Now, I want to know what you are doing here." It was Jim Baines.

"I was just playing a joke on someone." I couldn't quite get the words out. Besides, he should be able to tell for himself what was being done.

His eyes narrowed. "It seems to be a pretty malicious joke to me. Normally, I'd call it vandalism." He wasn't going to take this lightly. I didn't know what to say. I started to shake inside, and seemed frozen to the spot. He raised one eyebrow. "You're also breaking the curfew law." I didn't realize I had been gone that long. He motioned with his flashlight. "Get in the car."

I had to force myself to move. "What about my bike?"

"Bring it here." I quickly walked around the corner and wheeled my bike out. He picked it up and put it in the trunk. "Now, get in the car."

I wondered what he was going to do to me. The only contact I'd had with the police before was my Daddy. With him, I always knew he'd take me home. With Jim, I didn't even know if he recognized me from the picnic. He closed the door behind me. "I could take you straight down to the station and fill out a misdemeanor report."

Tears started to sting the backs of my eyelids. I didn't want to have a police record. "But, I'm going to take you home and we'll talk to your uncle about it."

At least he knew who I was. I wasn't sure which would be worse though, going to the station or being taken home. I fought back the tears. I had gotten myself into this mess; there was no reason for me to be a baby about it. "Are you going to charge me?" I wanted to know the worst before we arrived home.

He started the car. "Not this time. You're just lucky that I'm the one who caught you." I wasn't really sure about that. "If there is a next time, which there better not be, I won't just charge you." His voice got even deeper. "I'll put you in jail."

If I managed to live through this, I probably wouldn't do anything like it again. At least I'd be more careful about getting caught. I had been so worried about being caught by the family that I never thought about the police. We turned up the drive. I really dreaded going in the house this time.

"Come on." He strode up to the front door and knocked. I briefly considered hiding, but there was no place for me to go. I figured the best place for me to be was behind Jim. That way, I could avoid the initial anger of whoever opened the door.

"Jim! I thought you were on duty tonight." Sarah obviously didn't see me.

"I'm here on duty, Sarah. Is your Uncle in?"

"Sure." She sounded troubled. "Just a minute."

Jim turned around and grabbed my shoulder. He pushed me in front of him. I didn't have a chance to get nervous before Uncle Charley came to the door.

He looked at me and I could see the muscle along his jaw tighten. "It looks like you'd better come in." Jim did not let go of my shoulder as we walked into the house. It was getting a cramp in it from his grip. Matt, Mark, and Sarah were watching me from the living room. "What seems to be the trouble Jim?" His words were tight and short.

"I found your niece out by the Denton's house after curfew." He was starting with the least offense. "I noticed her behavior seemed to be a little strange, so I stopped and watched her for a couple minutes." I couldn't meet Uncle Charley's gaze anymore, so I looked at the ground. "She was taking Harvey's bike apart." Well, the worst was out now. "I decided to bring her here, instead of taking her down to the station."

Uncle Charley nodded. "Thanks Jim. I appreciate that."

The grip on my shoulder loosened slightly. "I figured it'd be easier for you since I'm not charging her with anything this time. And I knew you'd take care of the situation." That didn't sound too good for me. "As for you. . ." He turned me to stare into my eyes. "Just remember what I told you about repeating this." With a slight shake, he let go of my shoulder. "I'd like to think this whole thing was just one huge mistake. But, the only way to convince me of that is to never let it happen again."

I reached up and rubbed my shoulder to get the circulation going again. Uncle Charley shook Jim's hand. "Thanks again, Jim. I'll take care to see that this doesn't happen again."

Sarah walked Jim to the door, and I could hear them talking for a moment before he left. I didn't hear what they said because they spoke too softly. As soon as the door was shut, Uncle Charley sat me down in a chair.

"I'm going to ask you this question only once." Uncle Charley started pacing back and forth in front of me. "I want you to answer me straight. No beating around the bush." He paused to glare at me. "Did you dismantle Harvey's bike?"

I had never seen him so angry before. "Yes." I hardly choked out the word.

"Do you realize that is a crime?"

"Yes sir." Again the words came out softly. My throat had gone dry.

"Why on earth would you do something like that?" I put my hand in my pocket to fish for the note. "Well?"

It didn't look like Mark was going to come to my rescue this time. I didn't even want to see Matt. I knew exactly what his expression would be. My Daddy had worn that expression too many times. Uncle Charley continued to pace. "For as long as I can remember no McCabe has ever been on the wrong side of the law. You're not even here a week and the police are bringing you to the doorstep. I want to know why."

My fingers touched the edge of the note. "Harvey did something I didn't like."

Uncle Charley stopped pacing and closed his eyes for a moment. "What did he do?" His voice stayed quiet, but I knew that if I mouthed off in any way, he'd start yelling.

"I'll tell you, but you won't believe me."

His jaw tensed. "Katie, I'm trying to be as patient as I can with you, but you're making it difficult." He rubbed his temples. "You are going to be punished. No matter what reason you may have had for it, your action was wrong." He looked at the ceiling and took a deep breath. "I'd like a chance to understand why you did it though."

I pulled the note out of my pocket. "I didn't steal the master for the test. Harvey and Emma did." No one made a sound. They didn't believe me even now. "I have some sort of proof. Here." I handed Uncle Charley the note.

He read it through twice. "I'll take care of this tomorrow with your Vice Principal." That was it? He could have said he was wrong for not believing me.

"May I see it?" Sarah came over and he gave her the note. "Why didn't you show it to me before?"

"By the time I found it, I was so mad at you for not listening to me that it didn't seem to matter." I twisted my hands together. "Plus, I wanted to pay them back for getting me into so much trouble." Which now that I thought about it, didn't really work out all that well, because I was in more trouble now than I was before.

Uncle Charley sat down on the edge of his chair. "That's what I'm here for. They will take the blame for their actions." He'd better believe they would. "I'll make sure your school record is cleared."

Didn't he understand that I wanted more than that? "At the time, I was furious with them and with you. I knew it was wrong, but I thought it would make me feel better to fight back somehow." I did feel better about it, too bad I got caught. "When you didn't trust me to tell the truth, I didn't know what to do. Nothing I could say would change your mind. If I hadn't found that note, you still wouldn't believe me. I had to do something to make up for that."

Uncle Charley stood up again. "What you don't seem to realize is how serious this could have been." His hand ruffled up his hair. "If it had been someone other than Jim who caught you, you might have had a police record. I couldn't have taken care of that for you." He looked at his watch. "I want you straight home from school for the next two weeks. Sarah will let me know if you're late." Grounded again. "And all your privileges are taken away for that time."

I didn't have any privileges to begin with, so that wasn't a big deal. "All right." I turned to go to bed. Being grounded for two weeks wasn't that bad.

Uncle Charley put his hand on my shoulder. "Katie, I'd like you to come with me for a few minutes." Where did he want to go this time of night? "I think we should visit the barn before you go to bed."

I gulped and shoved my hands into my sweatshirt pockets. "Do we have to?"

"I'm afraid so." He opened the door and waited for me to go out first.

I had a sinking feeling I knew why he wanted us to visit the barn. "Uncle Charley, I'm sorry."

He put his hand on my head. "I know that." We went in the barn and he turned on the light.

"Then why do we have to do this?" My stomach was all knotted up.

He pulled out a tall three-legged stool. "Sit down." I was confused. I didn't think sitting down was in my immediate future, but I sat quickly so he wouldn't change his mind. He grabbed a shorter stool and sat down on it facing me. "I wanted to have a talk with you; just the two of us, where we won't be interrupted and no one else is listening in." He ran his hand through his hair. "We haven't spent any time together really, just the two of us."

His eyes looked sad. "I'm afraid we have gotten off on the wrong foot with each other. I've been having some rough work days and you have been having a rough time of things in general." That was putting it mildly. "A lot has happened in a very short time and your whole world has been turned upside down." He propped his foot on the rung of the stool. "I haven't been as understanding of that as I should have and I want you to know I'm sorry."

After all of the trouble I had caused him, he was apologizing to me? "Uncle Charley."

He held up his hand. "Let me finish what I have to say." He put his hand down on his knee and leaned forward. "Sam was my favorite brother. From the time he was born, he always looked up to me, and I feel like I have somehow let him down." A tear fell from Uncle Charley's eye. "He entrusted to my care the thing he treasured most in this world, and I feel like the events of tonight prove how much I have failed him." I was stricken as I watched the tear make its way down Uncle Charley's cheek. How could he think he was a failure? I was the one who was causing the problems. "You were right. I should have trusted your word instead of being so caught up in how it would look if I didn't discipline you." He took my hand and gazed straight into my eyes. "I was wrong, will you forgive me?"

I squeezed his hand. "Of course I will." The words came out in a whisper I was so choked up.

He gave me a sad smile. "Do you think we can wipe the slate clean and start all over again?"

"Yes." I jumped off my stool and flung myself into his arms. I buried my head on his shoulder and as he hugged me, I felt like I might never be able to let go. It felt so good to feel protected by his arms, to feel his love.

Time seemed to stop and I don't know how long he held me tight in his embrace before I felt a slackening in his grip. He spoke softly into my ear. "Katie, I want you to be able to come to me when you are having a problem with someone and trust me to help you deal with it." He pulled back so he could look into my eyes. "I know that I have let you down so far, but I promise I will be there for you from now on." He brushed some hair away from my face. "Okay?" I nodded. "So there won't be any need for you to try and handle things yourself. We'll do it together."

He stood up and patted me on the back. "Let's go to bed now and get a good night's sleep. Tomorrow will be a little easier to get through." He put his arm across my shoulders and we walked silently back to the house.

Sarah was all ready for bed when I walked into our room. "Are you okay?"

My face must have reflected the conflicting emotions I was feeling. "I don't know." I was having trouble sorting out my feelings.

"Is there anything I can do?"

I glanced at the window. The screen had been replaced. "I don't want to talk about it."

She nodded. "I understand." I put on my nightgown and crawled into bed. "I'm sorry Katie." I didn't say anything. "I know it's a little late, but I really am sorry for not believing that you didn't cheat on the test. We never had anything like that happen before. I didn't know how to react." She turned out the light.

"You could have tried believing me." It wasn't asking too much. "I don't tell lies, or steal, or cheat, you know."

Her voice softly penetrated the darkness. "No, I don't know." What was she talking about? "You've been here a few days, and in that time you were in a fight, ended up in the Vice Principal's office on the first day of school for unruly behavior and violence in a class, as well as getting detention in another class." Just what I needed to hear, a list of my sins. I could only see Sarah's outline as she leaned forward on her bed. "You also have bouts of being uncooperative and rude here at home. With all of that, you're asking me to know that you don't steal, cheat or tell lies?"

Maybe it was asking too much. "I understand that things are not easy for you right now." She came over to the side of my bed, knelt and put her hands on mine. "And that has a lot to do with why you are behaving the way you are." I felt tears well up in my eyes. My soul felt lacerated and my emotions raw. "I'm trying to get to know you Katie." Her voice had a sincerity to it that I could not doubt. "But, you've been working awfully hard at making that a difficult thing to do. I will trust you in the future."

The tears that I hadn't been able to cry while in the barn started sliding down my nose, and off onto my pillow. "I'm sorry Sarah."

She went over to the dresser and brought me some Kleenex. "Here. You don't want to sleep on a wet pillow."

I sat up and dabbed my eyes, and blew my nose. "I miss my Daddy so much I just don't know what I'm going to do."

She gave me a hug. "I know you miss him. You're sad, angry, hurt all at the same time. You've been uprooted from everything you're used to and your whole life has changed. That's a lot to adjust to, so we'll just have to take things one day at a time. Or sometimes it may be one moment at a time." She rubbed my arm. "For now though, I think you should try to get some sleep."

She crossed the room and got into her bed and I slid down in mine, but sleep seemed very far away.

Abducted

"Katie it's time to get up." I turned over and pulled the covers over my head. I went back to sleep without really waking up. "Katie." My eyes flew open. "I told you to get up ten minutes ago."

I buried my head in my pillow. "Leave me alone. I don't want to get up."

Sarah pulled back my blankets. "You don't have a choice. You have to get up for school."

I angrily threw the blankets the rest of the way back and sat up. "I told you to leave me alone. I'm not going to school." I couldn't believe how angry I felt. It seemed to fill me from head to toe and I didn't know where it was coming from.

Sarah opened the closet, pulled out an outfit for me to wear and put it on the top of the dresser. "I'll let you have a chance to get rid of your grouchiness. You'll have to hurry to get everything done in time." I threw my pillow at her as she went out the door. It missed, hitting the closed door instead.

My mood did not get any better. Little things kept happening that made me even angrier than before. When opening the dresser drawer, I missed the handle and jammed my finger into it. My fingernail broke so far down it started bleeding. The hens kept pecking at me from the moment I walked through the door of the coop until I left. I got soap in my eyes when I took a shower. The only day brightener was that Uncle Charley went into work early because of problems on the building. I'm not sure I could have faced him after our heart to heart the night before.

Even breakfast didn't go well. I reached for a piece of toast and knocked over my glass of orange juice. "I can't believe this! I can't take much more."

Sarah picked up the corner of the tablecloth so the juice wouldn't run on the floor. "Get a rag so we can get this cleaned up."

I pushed away from the table. "No. I've had it." I shoved the chair out of my way and it fell over.

"Calm down. There's no need to get so upset."

I was furious. "Maybe you don't have a reason." I glared at her. "But then you're wanted here. I'm not."

She folded the tablecloth up. "You're wanted Katie." She actually said it with a straight face.

"Don't make me sick." I went into the bedroom.

"Katie."

Why did she have to follow me everywhere? "Look. I'm only here because you feel sorry for me. Do you understand? That and Uncle Charley had to take me because my Daddy died." I started pulling my clothes out of my drawers. "I'm tired of being here, unwanted. But you wouldn't know about that, would you?"

Sarah took my clothes from me and put them back in the drawer. "Don't think you're the only one who had to leave home." I saw a spark of anger in her eyes. "When I came here to live, it wasn't exactly my choice either."

What was she talking about? "I'm here because my Daddy died, and no one else wanted me. Name something worse than that."

"My family had some financial problems and they picked me to leave home." There was a touch of bitterness behind her words. "Sometimes I still have a hard time dealing with it. Uncle Charley took me in, and for a long time I felt like I had to work in order to stay here." Her eyes were filling with tears. "I felt like a servant who had to earn her keep. But Uncle Charley kept on loving me until I felt like a part of the family."

He could do that for her, but it wouldn't work for me. I wouldn't be here that long for one thing. "He really wanted me to be here, just like he wants you to be here."

"That's what you think, but he's got you brainwashed." I tried to sound as insulting as possible because I wanted to lash out and hurt someone.

"Uncle Charley does care. You just have to give him a chance."

"Why should I?" He hadn't given me any breaks so far.

"He's been very concerned about you since your Daddy told him about his health." She paused for a moment to rub her forehead. "He wanted to make sure that you were provided for and looked after. He's the one who wanted you here."

"Stop it. I don't want to hear any more."

"Just because you don't want to hear it doesn't make it any less true." Her voice got sharp.

I started to leave the room, but Sarah grabbed my shoulder. "You want everyone to give you a break, but you aren't interested in giving anyone else one." She let go of my shoulder. "If you don't get ready right now, you'll be late for school." She was almost gentle when asking me to get ready and I expected anger.

I took the clothes from the top of the dresser and threw them on the bed. I was giving in to her again. I got so mad at myself when I did that. I didn't want to go to school, and if I stood my ground, she couldn't make me short of dragging me by force. But, instead I was getting ready anyway.

I had a headache, had to face Harvey and Emma in classes and had to put up with teachers' expectations and prejudices of me. I'd have to rush in order to make it to class on time. That meant I wouldn't be able to talk to Tom before classes. We never had a chance to talk in Geometry either because Mrs. Johnson loved to give detention for talking. Tom couldn't get detention because of football, and I didn't think it would be any fun either.

Leaving the house ten minutes later than I should have, I ran to the barn to get my bike. To top everything else off, the forecasted storm clouds were starting to form, which meant I probably got the joy of riding home in the rain. I rode as fast as I could hoping I could make up some of the time I lost arguing with Sarah.

I arrived at school out of breath and sweaty. At least I was on time, barely. Tom was on his way to class when he saw me. He came over to help me with my books. "What happened to you this morning?"

I must have looked horrible. "Sarah and I had another fight."

He stopped to hold the door open for me. "What about?"

"I don't have time to tell you about it now. We'll talk at lunch." I took my books back and went into class.

I made it through the door just before Mr. Whitehall closed it. Once the door was closed, you were considered tardy in his class. He only allowed three tardies before he sent you to the office. I sank into my chair, and leaned back against the wall to try and relax for a couple minutes. I needed to cool down.

I looked out the window while Mr. Whitehall began the review. He reviewed every morning what we had gone over the day before. I found it a big bore, so I never paid attention. The clouds kept getting darker and darker. It almost looked like the end of the day outside instead of first thing in the morning.

I saw Harvey walking across campus, grease streaked up his arms and on his face. It seemed like weeks ago when I dismantled his bike and I almost forgot what I had done. Jim must not have gone back to fix it. And no one else knew about his locker. I turned in my seat to see if I would be able to see him open it.

He paused to wipe his hands on his pants before turning the combination. He opened it quickly, and everything came spilling out in a glorious mess. Intent on watching Harvey, I didn't notice the class getting quiet.

"Is there something of interest out the window that you'd like to share with the rest of the class?"

I jumped in my seat. Mr. Whitehall was standing right next to me. "No."

"Then I suggest you turn around and pay attention to what is going on in this classroom." He went back to the front of the room. My face felt hot from embarrassment, and I slid down in my chair.

He seemed to enjoy putting me on the spot and making fun of me. "Now, Miss McCabe, since you are back with us, could you please tell the class what the three branches of government are, and what functions each branch has?" He knew I knew the answer, but he had to needle me a little more before going back to the boring old lecture.

When I got to second period, I wondered whether Emma had had any trouble with her bike and locker. She didn't have any grease on her that I could see. But, knowing Emma, I was sure that she would rather die before coming to class dirty. She definitely wasn't in a good mood, but that didn't say much. She never seemed to be in a good mood, unless she was trying to impress some grownup. Her book was wet though, so I knew the booby–trapped locker must have worked.

Since my plans came off so well, I started to feel a lot better about the day. I could handle being grounded for two weeks just knowing that Harvey and Emma had been paid back. One of the office girls came in with a note for Miss Phelps. I started to get paranoid every time I saw someone from the office because those notes always seemed to be for me or about me.

When Miss Phelps turned toward the class, I was half expecting to hear my name called. "Emma. Will you please come up here?"

Emma? Uncle Charley must have phoned Mr. Segerstrom. Harvey would be getting a similar note then too. This made my day. No matter how rotten yesterday was, and how much trouble I had gotten into, this was worth it. 'Little Miss Perfect' getting called into the Vice Principal's office. I just wished I could be there to hear them try and talk their way out of it. I couldn't wait until I had a chance to tell Tom everything that had gone on. I'd even risk the wrath of Mrs. Johnson to tell him about this.

After that, classes seemed to fly by. Almost before I knew it, Mrs. Johnson was dismissing us from class.

"What is going on with you today? This morning when I saw you, you looked like you were ready to explode. Now you almost got into trouble for telling me how happy you are." Tom raised his eyebrows. "So which is it? Happy or sad?"

"Right now, I'm so happy I could burst." I grabbed his hand and pulled him toward the benches. "I have so much to tell you, but this is just between you and me, all right?" He nodded. "Yesterday I got into a whole lot of trouble and I was ready to leave for good this morning." I took a bite of my sandwich.

He pulled his lunch out of the sack. "What was so bad it'd make you want to leave?"

I lowered my sandwich and looked at him. "That's what I'm trying to tell you."

"So what happened?" He unwrapped his sandwich.

"Harvey and Emma stole the master to the Geometry test and planted it on me." His eyes narrowed. "No one would believe that I hadn't done it. So I got mad and kind of wrecked their bikes."

"Katie." Tom didn't sound too pleased.

"Don't worry about it. All I did was take off their front tires." He shrugged and took another bite of his sandwich. "I got caught though. By Jim Baines." I looked down at the bench we were sitting on.

"Did he take you down to the station?"

I shook my head. "He took me home and Uncle Charley grounded me for two weeks." I traced the pattern of the wood. "So I won't be able to talk to you on the phone or hang out with you on the weekends." I looked back up at him. "But Emma got called into the office during second period, and Harvey wasn't there during fourth, so I know Uncle Charley must have talked to Mr. Segerstrom and told him about the note I found."

Confusion clouded his face. "What note?"

"I'm sorry, I forgot to tell you." Pausing for breath, I couldn't keep the excitement out of my voice. "I found a note from Harvey to Emma asking her about the test master." I grinned. "Now they're getting what they deserve. And that makes me happy." I started to eat my lunch again.

"I'm glad everything is working out." Tom paused and I wasn't sure if he was going to continue or not. "But, did you have to take apart their bikes? You could have gotten into a lot of trouble."

Not him too. "I know it was a stupid thing to do." He sounded so upset that I had to make him understand. "I was just so mad at them and at my family for not believing me, that I had to do something."

His eyes still looked pained. "Did Jim fill out a report when he caught you?"

"No. He just took me home and let Uncle Charley deal with me." I started twisting my lunch sack in my hands. "He let me know what could have happened though." I put the sack down.

"Just don't do anything like that again, okay?"

The pleading tone in his voice went straight to my heart. "Okay. I'll tell you what. If I have a problem with Harvey again, I'll talk to you before I do anything about it."

Relief spread across his face. "Great. So how much trouble are you in?"

I gave half a shrug. "Not much. I'm just grounded for the two weeks. You know how it goes. Home right after school, no friends over, and no phone calls." The buzzer sounded signaling the end of lunch.

"That's not too bad. I'll walk you to your next class."

The rest of the day sped by as quickly as the first part. I told Tom that I'd try to be at school a little extra early in the mornings. That way I'd have a chance to see him since I wouldn't be able to stay after school to watch him practice.

During volleyball, I kept looking at the sky to see if I could tell when it would start to rain. The air even had the smell of rain. The wind had picked up, and it kept carrying the ball to one side of the court.

As soon as the teacher said class was over, I ran to the locker room. I changed as quickly as I could and bundled my sweats into my locker. I wanted to get to my bike and home before the rain started to fall, if I could. The sky kept getting darker and darker. I would probably have to use the light on the bike to get home. Not to see, just to let the cars know that I was on the road.

Riding against the wind would make the trip home even harder. I grabbed the books I'd need for homework and threw them into my book bag. The wind kept whipping my hair in my face, and it tore at my clothes. Along with the wind, the sky started to spit tiny raindrops. It wasn't really raining yet, but it was close. I got out to the bike racks before anyone else, tossed down my book bag and picked up my lock.

Because of my hurry in the morning to get to class, I didn't watch where I dropped my lock. It landed combination side down in a grease slick. I carefully picked it up by the sides because I didn't want grease all over my hands and tried to twirl the combination. With the grease, the wind and my hands being cold, I kept dropping it. After three tries, I pulled an old homework paper out of my bag to clean off the lock.

I bent over the lock once more to open it. I wished the wind would stop, or at least die down a little because I was freezing. I didn't have enough sense to grab a jacket before I left in the morning. Mrs. Irwin must have let us out early because no one else seemed to be coming.

I finally got the combination done, and pulled down on the lock. A piece of cloth covered my eyes.

"What is going on here?" The blindfold tightened into place. I had been concentrating so hard on getting the lock open, that I hadn't heard anyone come up behind me. Somebody was playing a joke or it was some sort of freshman initiation, and I didn't have time for it.

I tried to stand up, but a pair of hands pushed me back down. "Hey! What are you doing?" A wad of material was shoved into my mouth, and another piece was tied around it to keep it in place. I tried again to stand up, this time with a lot more force. This joke wasn't funny anymore. Two pairs of hands pushed me back down.

I lost my balance, and ended up sprawled on the ground. Before I could move, my arms were yanked behind my back and my hands held together. Something like twine was then wrapped around my wrists and knotted. The twine cut into my flesh, and my arms had pain shooting down them. "Are you done yet?" The voice was a half whisper and sounded like a girl. If I could just see.

"No." Another knot was tied around my wrists. "I want to make sure she can't get out of this." This time the whisper was huskier, more like a boy's.

Before I could think it through any further, I was being pulled to my feet. I helped out just to get off the ground. I didn't understand why no one was coming to help me out, except for the fact that I left class early. Somebody would be coming soon though. There couldn't be that much time before classes were out.

Pushed in the small of my back, I had to take a step forward. I hoped that whoever was pushing me would be careful about where I stepped. Not being able to see, I felt like I was going to fall. I tried to remember the direction we took, so as soon as I got my hands free and was able to see, I'd be able to retrace my steps. We must have gone behind a building because the wind didn't seem so bad for a moment.

If there were only two people in this, especially if one was a girl and the other a boy, I knew it had to be Harvey and Emma. They were behind me, pushing when I didn't move fast enough for them, whispering about me. I couldn't quite hear what they were saying because of the wind.

I tripped as we stepped onto rougher ground and fell flat. A warm trickle down my leg told me that I must have skinned my knee when I fell. I rolled onto my back before they could get near me and kicked when someone got close. I landed one of my kicks.

"Stop it! I've got a dirty footprint on me now." Emma.

The next one landed in a soft stomach, so I knew that had to be Harvey. He wasn't stupid enough to talk out loud at least. He kind of grunted, and from the sound, he landed on the ground too. Then he ran around to my head before I could get myself turned around and ready to kick, and pulled me up by the arms.

It made me want to yell. But, I wouldn't give them the satisfaction of knowing that I had been hurt. I could hear and smell a horse near by. None of the houses right around the school had horses, and I knew we hadn't come far enough to be off school grounds. Horses were common in the area, but if there was someone on this horse, they sure weren't helping me out.

I ran into the horse because I had been pushed extra hard from behind. I felt like I got some horse hair up my nose. There was a growl in my ear. "Get on the horse." Even though he was trying to disguise it, the voice was unmistakably Harvey's.

How in the world was I supposed to get on the horse without being able to use my arms? Each one grabbed a leg and started pushing me up the side of the horse. I leaned against the side hoping I wouldn't fall and break something. I just hoped they had enough sense to stop pushing when I got to the top. I didn't want to fall off head first on the other side.

Just when I thought they weren't going to, they stopped pushing. Someone climbed up on the horse in back of me. The reins draped across my back, and the horse started moving. I couldn't believe they were making me ride this thing on my stomach. I wondered what they were going to try next. This was taking things a little too far.

From the way my clothes felt, it must have started sprinkling. The wind was still blowing strong, and it seemed to be getting colder by the minute. The person on the horse with me wheezed every once in a while, so I figured it must be Harvey. I only felt one person get on the horse with me though, so I wondered what Emma was up to. Before I had been angry, now I began to get a little frightened. I didn't know how far Harvey was going to take this revenge of his. And he didn't seem to be stopping.

We rode for so long that I lost track of time. I could tell we were going uphill from the slope. The ride was rough on me because Harvey didn't seem to want to walk the horse. He kept trying to get it to speed up. Every time the horse lurched forward, I thought I would fall off. Then, when my stomach hit again, I wished I had. At least that way I'd be off this stupid ride.

After what seemed like an eternity, Harvey brought the horse to a stop. He gave my shoulder a push to make me slide off the horse. I tried to go as slow as possible because I didn't want to fall when I landed. Harvey must have been getting a big kick out of seeing me helpless.

About halfway down I started sliding faster, and since I couldn't use my hands, I had no way of stopping myself or slowing down at all. My feet touched ground on some type of ledge. Because of my momentum, I couldn't catch my balance. I slid off the ledge into a river.

I landed flat on my back and the water covered me up completely.

The water rapidly soaked through my gag. Because I couldn't close my mouth the water kept pouring in, and I swallowed a lot of it. I thrashed around trying to stand up. My brain seemed paralyzed. I didn't know what to do. I couldn't breathe.

The bottom of the river was so slick that my feet couldn't get a good grip. By forcing my feet against the bottom and jumping up, I could get my head above the water. But with water in the gag, I still couldn't breathe. Panic filled me, and I was afraid that I might not be able to get out of the river.

One of the times I lifted my head, I could hear Harvey laughing. The sound of his laughter seemed to make something in my brain click. I stopped thrashing and rolled over, put my knees on the bottom of the river, and got my head completely above the water. Then I relaxed and breathed through my nose. I kept my head tilted forward, so the water would run back into the river.

My body felt weak from fighting the river and I stayed in the middle for a moment, glad to be able to breathe. They had tied the blindfold tightly enough that it didn't come off in the river. From the flow of the water against my body, I could tell which direction to go in order to get to the bank. Still on my knees, I cut across the current. I didn't know what I was going to do when I reached the side, but there had to be a way out.

I moved slowly so I wouldn't lose my balance and get swept under again. I was really fortunate to have fallen into a shallow part of the river. I couldn't have been under the water for too long. It just felt like I had swallowed a couple of buckets of water. I needed to cough and I felt like I was going to throw up, but with the gag in my mouth, I couldn't or I could end up choking on my own vomit. The ground was becoming a little firmer and I had to start climbing.

I ran into the bank. Now came the hard part, getting up the bank. I pushed myself against the bank and braced my feet on the ground. I had to wiggle back and forth and try to move forward. Once on top of the bank, I used my feet to push me away from the river.

The next thing I had to do was get my hands free. As I lay on the ground, my head to the side, I heard the clip-clop of horse hooves getting softer and softer. Harvey, the rat, was leaving me here like this.

I started tensing my wrists against the ties trying to loosen the twine. The twine swelled a little with the water. I tried crossing my wrists as much as I could and then jerking them out quickly.

Again and again I tried this. My arms were getting tired, and I was cold from being wet. I had no feeling left in my hands, and I was chilled through from the wind. Finally, the binding started to come loose. Thank goodness Harvey was not an expert at tying knots. As soon as I was able, I slipped one hand through the ties. It felt so good to be able to move my arms.

For a moment all I could do was move my arms trying to get the circulation moving again. Next I whipped off the blindfold and untied the gag. I crawled over to the edge of the river and vomited. I had to get all the water I had swallowed out of my system. I felt absolutely sick. After throwing up a couple more times, I washed my face off with some cool water. I rested on the ground for a couple of minutes more before even trying to get up.

When I got to my feet, I looked around. I had no idea where I was. Harvey brought me up into the hills somewhere, and I didn't have any idea of which way to go. I must have crawled to the opposite side of the river, because there didn't seem to be any horse trail or path near by. Tall trees stood all around, so I couldn't tell if there were any houses either. I shivered. The wind had not died down at all, and the sprinkles were starting to come down harder. I'd have to find a house somewhere. The only way to do that was to start walking.

If the sun were out, I could at least try to go in the direction of home. I checked my watch. My little dip in the river water-logged it and it stopped. It stopped at a quarter to four, so I knew it was past that and Sarah would be having a fit because I wasn't home from school yet. I could see me trying to explain this one to Uncle Charley. After our talk last night at least I had the hope that he might believe that I had been taken from school and left where I didn't know how to get back.

I started walking. My jeans felt heavy and rubbed uncomfortably against my legs. I reached down to squeeze some of the water out of them. I had a hole in the knee. It must have happened when I tripped before I got on the horse. My best pair too. I'd probably get into trouble for ruining my clothes. I figured my best bet was to follow the hill down. Sooner or later I'd have to get somewhere.

The brush started getting heavier and the trees thicker. I could no longer see my feet as I walked along. My body had goose bumps all over it from the cold. The slope was getting steeper, and I kept slipping on rocks and sticks that I couldn't see. At least I knew I was heading downhill. If the land leveled out, I could walk around in circles forever and never be able to find my way back.

Daddy had taken me camping several times, so I knew some things about staying out in the hills. But I didn't know enough to survive for any period of time. Especially if the storm broke before I made it to a familiar place. If that happened, I'd have to hole up somewhere until it passed through.

That could be until tomorrow or even later. Uncle Charley'd love that. They probably thought I ran away anyway, especially after my temper tantrum this morning. They'd be angry, but they wouldn't search for me very hard. My foot went through some twigs into nothingness and I fell forward.

I pulled myself along the ground before trying to stand up. Pain shot through my leg. I sank back down again. My body had smashed down enough of the brush when I fell so I didn't have to lift my leg in order to see my foot. I raised my pant leg and started to take off my shoe. My left ankle was so swollen I stopped. I didn't think I'd be able to get my shoe back on if I took it off.

I gently massaged my foot and ankle. It hurt every time I touched it, and I couldn't tell if I had broken it or not. From the way it looked it was probably broken though. Just what I needed. Walking around in the hills, freezing cold, not having any idea where I was, and now to top things off, I had a lame foot. My whole leg throbbed and I felt like crying. I just wanted to give up and not even try anymore.

While standing on my right leg, I managed to break off a tree limb. It wasn't the best kind of cane, but I had to have something to help me walk. I didn't even know how much farther I had to walk before I could find help. My pace had been slowed a great deal, and I was starting to feel tired. Since I only had one good foot, I seemed to slip a lot more in the mud too.

I had to be careful because the hill was getting rockier, and it had more pits like the one I hurt my foot in. I kept falling on miniature cliffs. Now I was not only soaked and chilled, but I was covered with mud. My clothes looked like a wreck too.

When I fell and hurt my foot, my shirt got caught on a branch and it ripped. I also had a bloody scratch on me from it. I would look like I had been through combat before I got home. At least it might help the family to believe my story. I slipped again and sat down hard.

I heard the rattle, but I didn't know where it was. The snake struck as I started to stand back up again. I lashed out with my stick, and beat it off. It escaped into some bushes before I had a chance to see what kind it was. I knew it was a rattler, but different kinds had different strength venom. I just hoped it wasn't a big old diamond back.

I had to get out of this brush and to a small clearing somewhere. I couldn't tell whether the snake had broken my skin or not. It had bitten the leg that was swollen and I couldn't feel much above the other pain anyway.

I started feeling sick to my stomach. My breath came faster and faster. There shouldn't have been a snake out with a storm coming and it was too cold. I didn't even think about watching for them as I tramped through the brush. To the side of me was a tree where the brush was a little lower. I had to get a look at the bite. My head started to feel fuzzy and my stomach more nauseous. I could almost hear Daddy telling me about snakes.

"If you get bit by a snake, the first thing to remember is not to panic." Panic was exactly what I was doing. "It just speeds up your heart rate and carries the poison through your body faster."

It was easy enough to say don't panic, but that didn't stop my heart from feeling like it was going to beat out of my chest. I brushed some hair away from my cheek, and my hand came away wet. I was crying and making little whimpering noises. I angrily brushed the tears away. I couldn't stop them.

I seemed to be moving in slow motion. I limped over to the tree and slid to the ground. I took some slow, deep breaths to try and calm myself down. Gently, I pulled up my pant leg.

"God, please don't let there be any bite marks." I looked down at my ankle. "Gross." It turned purple and was distorted. I looked carefully for bite marks. The two marks were there.

"No!" The sound dissolved into sobs. Why did all this have to be happening to me? Had I done something so terribly wrong? I couldn't tell if my ankle looked so bad because of the fall, the snake bite, or both. I didn't even know what kind of rattler it was. I tried to get a grip on myself and think things through.

"The first thing to do for a snake bite is. . ." My mind had gone blank. This was stupid. Daddy lectured me every time we went camping on what to do for snake bites. "I can't remember." Think of what Daddy used to say.

"Daddy! Where are you when I need you?" The wind tore my words from my lips and swirled them around. "Please God, help me to remember what to do." I didn't have much faith in prayer because I didn't have a very good track record of getting answers, but I didn't want to die alone on this hill. I had to remember.

"Help! Someone help me!" Maybe if I called loud and long enough, someone would hear me and come. I wiped my face again. I knew no one would hear me. I had to do it on my own. No one in their right mind would be out here in this weather.

"I don't want to die." I took a deep, shuddering breath. I knew that a snake bite needed medical attention and a shot of antivenin. "But I can't get to a doctor." What else could I do? If I walked on it without treating it somehow, the poison would spread faster. "Stop the poison." That had to be part of it. "Get some of the poison out." That was it. I had to get as much of the venom out of my system as I could.

"Bleed a snake bite." That was what my Daddy had told me to do. I had to hurry now because I had wasted a lot of time panicking. I searched for something to cut my leg with. I picked up a stick and tried it. "Not hard enough." I tossed the stick aside. "A rock ought to do it." I picked one that had an edge to it and began scraping at my leg. The pain was almost unbearable. I grit my teeth and kept trying.

"Not sharp enough." I threw the rock as hard as I could. There had to be something that I could cut myself with. Daddy had never allowed me to carry a pocket knife. He said they were dangerous and I could cut myself with one. I used to plead with him and promise that I would be careful and never cut myself. Now I wished I had one so I could cut myself on purpose.

I put my hand on my forehead. "My watch." It had a metal clasp. "It just might work." I fumbled with the catch. If this didn't work, I'd just have to try and suck the poison out the best I could. "Please God, let this work." I kept saying that over and over as I placed the side of my watch on my ankle. I braced my forefinger on it, pressed down, and scraped it across the bite. I closed my eyes and was afraid to open them up again.

"It worked!" A trickle of blood was running down my purple ankle. I quickly cut across the other mark. Then I leaned over and sucked the blood into my mouth. "Yuck." I spat it out on the ground. It tasted terrible. But, I had to keep sucking for a few minutes. I think Daddy told me five.

"What next?" I knew there was something else I should do before trying to walk on it. A tourniquet. "If only I hadn't thrown away the blindfold and the gag." I could have used them around my leg.

I ripped off the sleeve that had been torn anyway. Rain started pouring down. "Of course, I needed one more thing to help me out."

I tied the sleeve around my leg, just below the knee. I found a small stick and tied it down. Then I twisted it as much as I could. It hurt, but if I didn't get it tight, it wouldn't do any good. As soon as I had twisted it far enough, I ripped the sleeve on the sides and tied it in place.

"Time to get going." It was dark, and I couldn't see very far ahead, but I had to go. I couldn't stay in the hills all night with a snake bite. I picked up my makeshift cane and stood up. "Onward."

The pain was so bad, I almost fell over again. My knuckles went white as I gripped the stick, and I kept going. I had to keep track of the time somehow. I could only leave the tourniquet on for fifteen minutes and then I had to bleed the wound again. I wouldn't get anywhere fast, but I would at least get somewhere.

I wondered what they would be thinking at home. With the rain pouring down, I doubted that they would even try to look for me. They would probably be relieved that I hadn't come home. That way they could be rid of me and still say that they had tried.

"I'll give them what they want as soon as I'm better." I had to have two good feet in order to run away, so I'd have to stay long enough to let my ankle heal, if I ever got back of course. I didn't want to admit it, but I was scared. I knew I was doing the right things for the snake bite, but that was no guarantee that I would be able to survive. I still didn't even know where I was going.

I was wet completely through again, drenched from the rain this time. At least the wind wasn't quite as bad as it had been. I stopped and sat down on a fallen log to bleed my leg again. Every time I looked at my ankle, it was worse. I couldn't really see the color in the darkness, but it was swelling more and more. My tennis shoe would have to be cut off once I got to a doctor. After bleeding it again, and spitting out more poison, I got on my way again. My footsteps didn't seem to be as steady. My head was hot too.

"I have to keep going." I was getting nauseous again, but this time I knew it was from the poison in my system. At least the grade of the hill was lessening. I would slip enough on my own without that helping me. With the mud and rain, and a flimsy stick for support, walking on level ground would have been a chore. I started to feel very weak as I walked along.

"You can't give in to this." If I stopped, I might never get back up again. I still had to bleed my leg though. "Get your mind off it." Maybe if I did think of something else, I'd feel better. My thoughts went to my Daddy. Ever since he died, I kept thinking about things we had done together. I wanted him back. I still needed him.

I'd live forever with the picture of him standing there, tears streaming down his face, watching me out of sight for the last time. Maybe he thought he'd have more time. Then we could have faced his death together. I sat down to bleed my leg again. I guess I couldn't really blame Uncle Charley for what happened. I hadn't given him much of a chance.

My vision was blurring as I started out once again. My throat was dry, and felt a little swollen. I had to get somewhere soon. I couldn't go on much longer. I stumbled more with every step, and had to pause a lot. I had let too much of the poison get into me.

"A light." Something glowed in the darkness. It disappeared as I lurched from side to side, but I had a goal now. With a last surge of strength, I headed toward the light. The light seemed to call to me. Every part of me was straining to get to it. It was like it had a life of its own. Swinging from side to side, almost like a fairy light.

I stumbled again and ended up in the mud. I lost my stick as I fell and I couldn't find it. Not able to stand up without something to lean on, I pooled my strength and started crawling. The light was not far off now, and I could tell that it was shining out of a window. I drug myself through the mud toward the house. A shadow passed across the light. I was so excited I could hardly contain myself. I wanted to yell for joy. Someone was home. I would have help at last.

I pulled myself up to a standing position on the edge of the porch. All I had to do was walk across it and knock on the door. I tried to put weight on my lame leg, but it didn't want to work. Steeling myself for one last effort, I stepped out. I fell against the wall of the house when I got there, but I had made it. I used the wall for support, raised my hand and rang the bell.

On the Home Front

S arah looked at the clock. Twenty minutes after three. Katie should have been home ten minutes ago. Tossing the dish towel in the sink, she opened up the freezer. She really thought that Katie had listened to Uncle Charley this time, and would have come straight home. Maybe she had been delayed for some reason. "I hope she's not goofing off or getting into trouble again."

Oh well, she'd give her a few more minutes before calling her late. Uncle Charley had asked that she keep track of Katie when he wasn't home, and Sarah wondered how she was supposed to do that when Katie didn't show up. Pulling out a pan for the roast, Sarah looked out the window. From the looks of the sky, Uncle Charley might have to knock off work early because of the weather. It was early in the year for storm clouds to be gathering. Uncle Charley had been hoping to get the exterior work on the building done before the rainy season came.

Sarah put the roast in the oven, looked at the clock and frowned. "Katie, you're late. And I don't have time to go out and look for you either." The wash she had done earlier was still out on the line. Sprinkles started hitting the ground. Sarah grabbed the laundry basket and ran outside.

"Oh no." The wind had blown some of the clothes onto the ground and they would have to be re-washed. If Katie had been home on time like she was supposed to be, she could have helped out. The wind tried to tear the clothes out of Sarah's fingers as she took them off the line. She kept glancing toward the drive hoping to see Katie wheeling in.

Once the clothes were gathered and in the house, Sarah started shutting things up. The animals were still out in the pasture, and needed to be brought in. Mark had taken Günter along to help guard some of the material at work. Since Günter usually helped herd the animals at night, Sarah would be short-handed again.

Bossy was easy enough to bring in. Sarah just put the halter on her and led her back to the barn. Getting the sheep back to their pen turned out to be a different story. Every time she got close, they would run off. The blowing of the wind seemed to have spooked them. The rain was starting to come down, and Sarah had forgotten to wear a raincoat. He blouse clung to her skin as she tried to catch the sheep.

She managed to grab one, but couldn't hold it, or pull it toward the gate because there was nothing to hold on to except skin and wool. The sheep was so scared anyway that it jerked and ran. Sarah let go before getting pulled into the mud. A bolt of lightning brightened the sky. When the thunder sounded the already frightened sheep started running into one another. From the direction of the house came barking.

Sarah turned around. "Thank goodness." Mark had come home bringing Günter with him. "Mark. I'm out here." She waved her arm. He had been heading toward the house. He bent down and said something to Günter. The dog raced over to the pasture. Mark followed, not far behind. "I didn't think I'd ever get any help tonight."

Mark looked around. "So where's Katie? She should be helping out."

Sarah shook her head. "She hasn't come home from school."

Mark opened the gate and walked in. "Where is she?"

She shrugged. "I don't know. I'm a little worried. She should have been home a long time ago."

He gently pushed her toward the gate. "You go in the house and see if she's back now. I'll take care of the sheep and be in, in a few minutes." He patted her shoulder. "Don't worry. We'll find her."

Don't worry. That was easy for him to say. She couldn't help it. It was almost four-thirty. Katie should have been home well over an hour ago. Sarah went around to the back door so she didn't drip all over the entryway. "Katie? Are you home?" No answer. Even if she had gotten a flat tire and had to walk home, she would have been back by this time. Sarah changed into some dry clothes. The front door closed with a bang. "Katie, is that you?"

"No. The sheep are in though." Sarah walked into the living room. Mark ran a hand through his wet hair. "She's not back then?"

She shook her head. "I don't know what to do Mark. I don't know whether she's deliberately staying away, or if she's in some kind of trouble." She bit her lip. "That storm is going to break any minute. I just wish I knew where she was."

"Take it easy. I'll go look for her."

Picking up the telephone receiver, Sarah started dialing.

"What are you doing?"

"Calling Jim."

Mark pushed down the button, cutting the connection. "I think you should wait until Dad gets home before doing that." He took the receiver and placed it back on the hook. "He and Matt should be home any minute."

Sarah started getting angry. "What if she's run away? The longer we wait the less chance we have of getting her back."

Mark frowned. "Why would she run away?"

"The past couple days haven't exactly been the easiest for her. She almost took off this morning." She jerked the receiver off the hook. "I'm calling Jim." Mark reached out to push the button down again. "Don't even think about it, Mark." He pulled his hand back. "If she comes home, I can always call back."

Flopping into a chair, Mark scowled across the room. Sarah turned her back. "Hello Jim? Are you working tonight?"

"You know I work the weeknights."

Relieved she continued. "Katie hasn't come home from school yet, and I'm afraid something may have happened to her." She started pacing back and forth. "She also might have run away."

"Because of her age, I can't officially do anything." She had counted on Jim being able to help. "But I'll see what I can find out for you."

With a sigh of relief Sarah sank into a chair. "Thanks Jim."

"I go on duty at five. Stay by the phone, and I'll let you know as soon as I find anything out."

She stood up again. "Thanks again, Jim. I'll let you know if we find her, too." She hung up the phone and turned toward Mark. "He's going to keep us posted."

He got to his feet and grabbed his jacket. "I still think you should have waited for Dad to get home."

Sarah heard the cars in the drive. Then the door opened and Matt walked in.

"Where are you going? I didn't think I'd ever see the day that you'd skip out on supper." Uncle Charley wiped his feet on the mat, and then walked in.

Mark pulled out his car keys. "Katie hasn't come home from school yet and I'm going to look for her."

Matt put his coat back on. "I'll go with you."

"Wait a minute." Uncle Charley closed the door. "Before anyone leaves, we need to figure out what we're doing." He turned toward Sarah. "Did you call Jim?"

"I just finished talking to him." She knew despite Mark's objections she had done the right thing.

He nodded. "Good. Then I want you to stay here and wait for any phone calls." He rubbed his forehead. "We have to consider the possibility that she has run away, so she may not be in the open."

Mark shoved his hands in his pockets. "I don't see why you would automatically think that she'd run off."

"She's tried it before, even while at home with Sam, and she probably thinks she has more reason to run now." Sarah knew that Mark really didn't believe that. The phone rang.

"I'll get it." Matt strode over and picked it up.

"Mark, I want you and Matt to make a search of the east section of town. Take the school and look around the lake."

"Dad." Matt held out the receiver. "It's Tom Pike. He's a friend of Katie's and I think you should talk to him."

Tom was the one Katie had spent so much time with at the picnic. Maybe she stayed after school to be with him. She'd have to talk to Katie when she got home to see how serious this friendship was. Something told her that it may be the beginning of more than friendship, and Katie was too young to be dating yet. It had only been a week though. Things couldn't have gone that far.

"After leaving practice, Tom saw Katie's bike still at school. He was calling to make sure she had made it home all right." Uncle Charley opened the door. "Make sure you check the school area well. Tom says that he knows Katie was planning on coming straight home."

Sarah was puzzled. "How would he know that?"

He shrugged. "Apparently she told him she had to." Matt and Mark left. "Call Jim and tell him about the bike. We'll call every half hour."

The door closed and silence filled the house. She couldn't just sit by the phone and wait for it to ring, and she would have to wait for a few minutes before getting in touch with Jim. The roast. If the heat didn't get turned down, it would be dried out and charred. Turning the oven down to warm, Sarah looked around the kitchen to see what she could do. Now might be a good time to clean out the refrigerator. It wouldn't take a whole lot of thought, and she would be able to leave it easily. She checked her watch. Jim would be at work now.

"Sheriff Department, Jim Baines speaking."

Good. He was on duty. "Hi, Jim. I'm just calling to let you know what's going on. Matt, Mark, and Uncle Charley are out looking for Katie right now." She grabbed a scarf and tied it in her hair. "A friend of hers called because her bike was still at the school. He also said that she had planned to come straight home."

"All right. I'll check out the school. Thanks for calling Sarah."

Back to cleaning the fridge. Every sound made her jump. The rain started pouring down, and Sarah kept going to the door and staring out into the night. Worried before because she though Katie had run away, Sarah was even more frightened now that it looked like she hadn't.

Anything might have happened to her. With the rain and the wind, they wouldn't be able to see very well, and she might be hiding somewhere to get out of the rain.

One shelf down, three more to go and a couple drawers. She looked over at the phone. "Ring."

Time seemed to be crawling by. If the phone didn't ring soon, she thought she'd go crazy. Another shelf cleaned. Now the stuff had to be put back in. Sarah got a glass of water and looked out the window again.

The phone rang. Sarah dropped the glass of water and it shattered all over the floor. "I can't believe I did that." The phone rang again. Sarah ran over to it. "It's probably just Uncle Charley calling in to say that he hasn't found her yet." She took a deep breath and picked up the phone. "Hello."

"Is this the McCabe house?" A woman was speaking on the other end.

"Yes, it is." If this was a salesperson, Sarah thought she would scream.

"This is Mrs. Dryer. I live on Sycamore Avenue." It didn't sound like a sales pitch. "A girl knocked on my door."

"Katie?"

There was a pause on the other end. "Why yes." Mrs. Dryer sounded flustered. Sarah decided to keep quiet until she finished this time. "I heard a knock on my door this evening, and I couldn't figure out who it could be." Sarah bit her lip to keep from trying to hurry her up. "I wasn't expecting any visitors, and no one I knew would have been dropping by to see me with the rain pouring down like this."

How maddening. Would the woman ever get to telling her about Katie? "Well anyway, I answered the door and this girl, who was completely caked with mud, practically fell in the door." Caked with mud? Maybe she had fallen down in the rain. "I had to help her inside because she couldn't walk." Something was wrong with her. Sarah's heart started beating harder. "The poor thing has a fever so high she can hardly talk. She kept telling me something about her leg and a snake. I really can't make out what she's trying to tell me." She must really be hurt.

"She gave her name and this number to call. I think she needs a doctor."

At last a time to break in. "I'll call one as soon as I hang up. Would she be able to talk to me?"

"I think she might be able to."

Good. If she could hear Katie, and have her explain what happened, then she'd know what kind of help to bring. "What's your address on Sycamore, Mrs. Dryer?"

"1661."

Sarah scratched it down on a piece of paper. She'd call Jim and a doctor as soon as she hung up. "Thank you for calling me, Mrs. Dryer. May I talk to Katie now?"

"Certainly."

The wait seemed to take forever. "Sarah?" Her voice sounded so weak.

"Katie. What happened?"

Arrival of the Cavalry

I leaned against the side of the house while I waited for someone to answer the door. I had my finger on the bell ready to push it again when I saw a shadow loom up behind the door.

The door creaked slowly open and a white face bobbed in front of me. "Oh my goodness. What happened?" I tried to answer, but the words wouldn't come out. "Well, come in out of the rain." She was little. I took a step forward and fell to my knees. "Oh dear!" She reached down and tried to help me up. She was old and had white hair, so she couldn't give me much support. Somehow we managed though.

"We need to set you down somewhere." The nearest possible chair would be good. "But I don't want to put you in the living room. I might not be able to get the mud out of the upholstery." All I wanted to do was collapse, and this lady was thinking about upholstery. "The kitchen would be the best place. There isn't any carpet to worry about in there either."

I didn't care as long as I could sit down soon. I could die before she made up her mind where I could sit. "My name is Mrs. Dryer. Is there anything I can get you?"

My throat hurt and was dry. "Water." I thought I'd never want another drink after all the water I swallowed in the river. That seemed like it happened in another age.

"Would you like ice in that?" I shook my head. All I needed was something to wet my throat so I could talk. "Here you go. Now, tell me what happened to you."

I sipped the water. It felt nice and cool. "I'm Katie and I need help. Call Sarah." I couldn't tell her the whole story. For one thing it would take too long, and she didn't need to know it for another. I just needed some help. Sarah would be at home at least, and she would come for me.

"Here. Let me wipe off your face. It's dirty." No kidding. So was everything else. "My goodness. You have a fever." I had guessed that, but now it was confirmed. "I think we should get you a doctor."

"No." I needed to call home first. They would take care of me. I didn't even have a doctor here. "I need to call home."

"That's fine, Dear. I'll make the call for you. You just rest." She bustled out of the room, and then returned quickly. "If you'll write your name and phone number down, I'll call and have your family come get you."

At last I seemed to be getting somewhere. I wrote it down and tried to tell her at the same time things to tell Sarah. "My leg is hurt." Talking was still hard. I couldn't seem to write and talk at the same time either. "The snake got my ankle."

"That's fine, Dear. Just rest now."

I wished she would stop calling me dear, as if it were my name. I didn't like that. She called from the kitchen. I must have written the numbers too small or something because she kept looking at the paper before dialing each one. Finally, she was talking to someone. She seemed to be giving the complete history of my showing up at the door. If I weren't so sick, I would have been irritated. She turned toward me. "She'd like to talk to you."

Good, I could at least tell her the highlights without them getting garbled. She brought me the phone. "Sarah?" The word caught in my throat.

"Katie, what happened?"

I'd have to give the shortened version. "I only have time to tell you the important things." I took another sip of water. "I've been bitten by a rattler."

"What?" She was not being calm.

"It'll be all right. I think I broke my ankle too. I just need you to come get me." My voice broke a little on the last words. I was tired of being strong.

"I'll be there as soon as I can. I'm going to call Jim as soon as I hang up." He'd be thrilled to see me again so soon. "I'll have him bring a doctor. I have to wait here until Uncle Charley calls in. Then I'll be right over." She sounded so worried. "Rest until I get there." I couldn't move if I wanted to. "Don't argue with the doctor. Bye now."

"Good-bye." I hoped she hurried and got here. I didn't want to stay here in pain for very much longer. It was such a relief to know that I didn't have to do anything more. I had made it to a house and help was on the way.

"Let's see if we can get you cleaned up a little, Dear."

I was in agony, and she wanted to clean me up. "I'd rather wait until someone came for me." I didn't want to be moved.

"Well then, why don't we put your hurt foot up?" She reached down and tried to pick it up.

I screamed. "Let me keep it down. It'll be better for it anyway."

"But it's so swollen. It needs to be elevated for the swelling."

That was true, and the swelling wasn't the only thing wrong with the leg. "It hurts too much to put it up." She nodded and opened her mouth to say something. I broke in before she got the chance. "I'd like to wait until the doctor gets here. He's coming with the deputy."

"Oh? Why is a policeman coming?"

I shouldn't have said anything about Jim. "He's my cousin's boyfriend. He's bringing the doctor. Sarah's coming as soon as she can."

"Well, that's all right then." She paused. "Were you on a walk and just got caught in the storm?"

You could say that. I certainly got caught in something. "I guess I kind of lost my way."

I heard a siren wailing outside. Jim must be coming. How embarrassing. I was glad that no one from school was around. At least he would be bringing a doctor. The doorbell rang repeatedly and someone pounded on the door.

"That must be your friends." Who else would it be? She had to go into a long explanation on the phone to Sarah about how she wasn't expecting anyone. "I'll answer it dear. You just sit right there." How in the world was I supposed to even think about getting up to answer the door? I couldn't walk without help.

"Where is she?" That sounded like Jim.

"She's out in the kitchen." I heard Jim's boots pounding on the wooden floor, but Sarah came through the door first.

"I thought you had to wait for Uncle Charley to call."

She stopped when she saw me. I was going to have to put up a tough front. She looked like she might cry. "Katie."

"I'm all right. I bet I'm better off than the snake." Jim came into the room. I lifted my hand in greeting. "You still didn't tell me what you're doing here."

Sarah stayed rooted to the spot. "Jim radioed Uncle Charley and came and picked me up." Jim knelt by my foot and gently pulled up the pant leg to look at the foot. I grit my teeth to keep from crying out. The color started coming back to her cheeks. "The doctor was on another call, but he'll be here within fifteen minutes."

I could wait that much longer. I had made it this far. "Uncle Charley said that he'll come as soon as he gets a hold of Matt and Mark." Pretty soon the whole gang would be here to watch me suffer. Sarah took a deep breath. "Jim, let me see it."

He glanced up at her. "Are you sure you want to, honey?"

She nodded. "The doctor told me to look for certain things." I heard her take a sharp breath and let it out slowly. It must look pretty bad by now. It looked bad enough when I could see it, right after it got wrecked up. "This is awful. Is it all from the bite?"

"No." I had to breathe slowly because it hurt again. "I fell and twisted it before it got bit."

She patted my leg. "I'm afraid you may have done more than twist it."

I didn't want her to say that. "Are you sure? I don't want it to be broken."

Sarah pulled a chair next to mine. "If it is broken, we'll take care of it." She took my hand. "It won't be fun, but you'll survive it."

Survive. I guess I would, but it wouldn't be any fun trying to get around on crutches. "While we're waiting for the doctor, why don't you tell me how you managed to be up in these hills?"

I knew that had to be coming. What could I say? "I was going to come home right after school." I had to make sure she knew that.

"I know. Tom called to tell me that your bike was still at school."

Thank goodness for that. "Harvey, with Emma's help, took me from school, threw me into a river, and left me."

I wouldn't tell her about being tied up, gagged, and blindfolded, at least not yet. The experience was too horrible for me to deal with still. "I didn't know where I was, or how to get home." I turned my head. Sarah looked so angry that I couldn't face her anymore. "I slipped as I was walking down the hill. There was some kind of hole I stepped in. And then I got bit by the snake." That about summed everything up.

"Did you do anything for the bite?"

I nodded. "I bled it every fifteen minutes, and put a tourniquet on it." How easy that sounded. How terrified I was when I had to do it.

There was a knock at the door again. Mrs. Dryer went scuttling out to answer it. I was surprised that she didn't interrupt us while we were talking, asking us if we wanted tea, or anything like that. The doctor arrived, and I saw Uncle Charley in the doorway right behind him. I smiled and gave a weak wave.

The doctor looked around. The kitchen had become too crowded for everyone. "I'd like the kitchen cleared out, please."

Sarah started to get up. "Will you stay with me?" She looked at the doctor and he nodded. Everyone else went into the living room.

The doctor sat down next to me. He radiated efficiency. "Now then, let's see what we've got here." He could look. I didn't want to. "It looks like you've got yourself a pretty nasty injury here." I grabbed onto Sarah's hand as the doctor probed my ankle. "The first thing I'm going to do is give you a shot of antivenin."

I hated shots. He pulled out the needle, filled and prepped it. I buried my head on Sarah's shoulder as he gave it to me. "Ouch."

"Well, that wasn't much of a yell." I could yell louder if he wanted me to. "I'd like you to go into the hospital for observation." The hospital. "I don't know how far the poison has gone into your system." He put the syringe back in his bag.

"No." I clutched Sarah's arm. Panic crept into my voice. "I don't want to go to the hospital."

She looked at the doctor. "If you tell us what to do, we'll make sure that she's well taken care of at home."

The doctor scowled for a moment. "I guess I can trust you to watch her. If the fever doesn't break by tomorrow morning, give me a call." He took some scissors and cut away my tennis shoe. "I want her to come into the office tomorrow anyway." He started wrapping my foot in an ace bandage. "I'll need x-rays on this foot. Until then, she needs to stay off of it, keep it iced, fifteen minutes on and fifteen minutes off, and elevated to take down the swelling." It was just one more ordeal to go through. I couldn't believe that Sarah stuck up for me about staying at home though. Maybe she did care about me after all. "She'll be in a lot of discomfort until the venom gets out of her system. She needs to drink plenty of liquids."

If I could manage this far, a little more pain wouldn't be too bad. "Can we take her home now?" He nodded. "Uncle Charley? Jim? We're ready to go."

They came in and picked me up. "We'll carry you to the car." How fun. A chair of hands to sit on. At least I didn't have to try to hop.

Sarah stayed right by my side as they carried me out. "We'll get you home, cleaned up, and into bed. Then I'll tell Uncle Charley what happened. He'll want to know, but you need your rest."

We arrived at the police car and they set me down. Sarah got in the car with me while Jim and Uncle Charley went to talk to Mrs. Dryer for a few minutes. "Sarah? Did you think I had run away?" Part of me didn't want to ask because I knew what the answer would probably be, but I needed to know for sure.

She looked down at her hands. "I thought it was possible." That's what I thought. I turned and looked out the window. At least she had been honest about it. "Especially after our argument this morning. But, I was hoping you hadn't."

My head snapped around. "Really?"

She nodded. It gave me a warm feeling inside to know that she hadn't wanted me to be gone. It would have been a lot easier for her if I had left. With as mean as I had been to her, it wouldn't have surprised me if she hoped I had run away. The drive home was quiet. Sarah kept peering anxiously at me through the darkness. "Why do you care so much?"

She squeezed my hand. "Because I love you."

I didn't try to argue with her this time like I would have if she had said the same thing to me this morning. My leg still hurt, but it was nice to lean back and know that I was loved. The car pulled into the driveway and Matt and Mark came running over. They had been waiting for us to drive up.

"Is she all right?" The concern in their voices was evident. For some reason I didn't feel like I had to gain their love, I knew I had it already.

Sarah got out of the car. "She needs to be carried into the house. She shouldn't walk on that foot right now."

Things started to become dream-like, not real. Probably from the pain in my leg and the fever I had. I remember Uncle Charley checking on me and making sure that I was being taken care of. He really seemed to care. I heard him talking to Jim about Harvey, but I couldn't hear enough of the conversation to make any sense out of it. Normally, I'd have been dying to know what was going on, but it didn't matter a whole lot to me. What mattered was the attention and care I was receiving.

Uncle Charley came in after Jim left. He sat down beside me. "Katie, I don't understand how you and Harvey got to be enemies so fast. But, this revenge cycle that is going on between the two of you is stopping right now." He held my hand. "We've just come very close to losing you, and I don't want to get within shouting distance of this kind of experience again." It wasn't something I wanted to do again in a hurry either. "I just want to be sure that you understand that you are not to attempt any sort of revenge against Harvey or Emma for this." He cleared his throat. "It's time you let me handle the situation. Agreed?" I nodded. "Good. I want you to get some rest now and I'm going to call some parents and let them know how serious this was."

After cleaning me up and tucking me in bed, Sarah pulled a chair over. "I'll just watch you for awhile."

I nodded, my eyes getting heavy. "It's good to be home." She smiled and brushed my hair off my forehead as I fell asleep.